'Of course I care, and not just because you're a colleague or because it's the professional thing to do. I care because I *care* for you. *Deeply.*'

'How deeply?' He gazed down into her eyes. 'Deeply enough to take a chance?'

Jake looked down into her eyes before a small smile tugged at his lips. When had it happened? How had she become so incredibly special to him in a matter of weeks?

'Bek.' He lowered his mouth to hers, intent on showing her that he, too, cared for her.

PRACTISING AND PREGNANT

**Dedicated doctors, determinedly single—
and unexpectedly pregnant!**

These dedicated doctors have one goal in life—to heal
patients and save lives. They've little time for love, but
somehow it finds them. When they're faced with single
parenthood too how do they juggle the demands and
dilemmas of their professional and private lives?

PRACTISING AND PREGNANT

Emotionally entangled stories of doctors in love
from Mills & Boon® Medical Romance™

HIS
PREGNANT GP

BY
LUCY CLARK

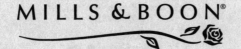

MILLS & BOON®

To DJ—thanks for sharing your knowledge.
Hebrews 13:5

First published in Great Britain 2004
Harlequin Mills & Boon Limited,
Eton House, 18-24 Paradise Road, Richmond, Surrey TW9 1SR

© Lucy Clark 2004

ISBN 0 263 83896 X

Set in Times Roman 10½ on 12 pt.
03-0504-48705

Printed and bound in Spain
by Litografía Rosés, S.A., Barcelona

CHAPTER ONE

'I SHOULD demand a step stool in every aisle if they want me to continue to shop here.' Rebekah stood on tiptoe, stretching as high as she could to the top shelf. 'Nope.' She relaxed back with a sigh and rubbed the large bump of her stomach. 'It may help, baby, if you didn't continue to stab me with your elbows. Hmm? How about giving Mummy a break?'

She stepped back to look at the item she wanted with longing.

'Excuse me.'

Rebekah turned at the deep, rich voice which had mildly startled her. Her gaze came face to face with hard, muscled chest hidden beneath a navy polo shirt. Slowly, she lifted her gaze to his face. He was frowning and she wasn't sure why. Never mind, he was here…and he was tall!

'Hi. Would you mind getting me that bag of coffee beans, please? The red one.' She pointed. 'There are a few at the back but how they expect me to get them in my condition is beyond me.'

He quickly obliged—not even stretching—and handed her the coffee. The woman was about five feet three and she looked to be about eighteen years old, especially with her black hair tied in pigtails. They hung over her shoulder with red ribbons tied on each end and for some reason he thought they were…cute.

'Thanks.' She smiled brightly and dumped it into her disorganised grocery trolley.

'You're welcome.' He looked at the coffee and then

pointedly at her 'bump'. 'Should you be drinking coffee in your condition?'

'Oh, not you too. I'm perfectly fine and so is my baby. It's the one luxury I refuse to do without and I'm only having one very mild cup a day.' She rubbed her baby absent-mindedly. 'I need *something* to get me going in the morning, especially after Junior here does aerobics most nights.' She checked her list again. 'Thanks for your help.' With that, she started pushing her trolley down the aisle.

'Uh…sorry.' She turned as he spoke. 'I'm looking for Dr Sanderson. The lady at the checkout told me she was in aisle eight.'

Rebekah looked up at the sign above her. 'Yep. Aisle eight, all right. So what can I do for you?'

'Pardon?' His eyes widened in stunned amazement. No! This heavily pregnant woman could not possibly be Dr Rebekah Sanderson. Jake's shock turned to horror as he continued to stare at her. His gaze dropped to her pregnant stomach before returning to meet her happy, smiling face. His new colleague was pregnant! No one had mentioned *that* fact to him when he'd accepted the locum position. 'Uh…' He looked up and down the aisle again, positive this had to be a mistake. There was no one else around.

'Hello?'

He cleared his throat and pulled himself together. 'Jake Carson.' He raked a hand through his hair, looking expectantly into her blue eyes. She couldn't possibly be eighteen years old. He looked for telltale wrinkles and character lines, trying to gauge just how old she was.

'Oh, hi.' Rebekah held out her hand. His own was warm and the shake was direct and firm. 'I wasn't expecting you until this evening.' She gestured to her shopping trolley. 'Hence the reason for this last-minute shop. There's nothing in the cupboards.' Why, all of a sudden, did she feel so self-conscious? Perhaps it was because she was faced with very tall, very dark and *very* handsome stranger with the most amazing blue eyes she'd ever seen. A stirring of something foreign sizzled in her tummy and it definitely wasn't indigestion! He frowned and she flicked her pigtails back over her shoulders. 'Problem?'

'Why should it matter if there's nothing in the cupboards?'

Rebekah shrugged and glanced at her watch. 'Yikes. Is that the time?' She started pushing the trolley. 'I guess I like to eat food when I get home from work. I naturally presumed you would, too.'

He fell into step beside her. 'I don't follow.'

'Your lodgings. They're the other half of my house. We share a kitchen, laundry and living room.'

'Bathroom?'

'No.' Her smile broadened. 'You're out of luck,' she teased. 'The bedrooms, with *en suites*, are at opposite ends of the house. I'm quite proud of it. We only finished the renovations last week.'

'We?' He glanced down at her left hand on the trolley—no wedding ring.

Rebekah saw his interested look. 'I'm a widow. The ''we'' I was referring to is myself and Bert, the builder.' She turned into the next aisle and checked her list again. She looked at the shelves and then lifted a hand dejectedly. 'Why is everything on the top shelf today? I swear it's a conspiracy to stop pregnant women from getting what they want. Jake, would you mind getting that jar of pickles down, please?'

'Cravings?' Reaching up, he needed to move a little closer to her and as he did, the subtle scent of roses filled his senses.

Rebekah grinned again. 'Oh, yeah. Pickles and bananas are high on the list at the moment.'

'Your body must be low in sodium and potassium.'

'Very good, Dr Carson.' She added a few more things to the trolley, checked her list and nodded. 'That's it…unless there's something you'd really like.'

He thoughtfully scanned the contents of the trolley. He was on a strict, low-cholesterol diet specifically designed to help lower his blood pressure. 'I'll come and get it if I need it.'

'OK.' She headed for the checkout.

'Ah-h, I see you found her,' the checkout lady said to Jake as Rebekah started to unload the trolley. The baby kicked and Rebekah groaned, rubbing her stomach. The next instant, her phone started to ring.

She pulled the mobile out of her pocket and connected the call. 'Dr Sanderson. Yes, Nicole. I'm on my way.' She lifted a large tub of ice cream out of the trolley, almost dropping it, but thankfully Jake caught it. 'Thanks,' she said softly. 'I can't live without ice cream at the moment. Pardon, Nicole?' She paused and then looked at Jake. 'Yes. Yes, he found me. We'll head back to the house so I can put the shopping away and then we'll come to the clinic. OK. See you then.' She disconnected the call. 'That was Nicole, the clinic receptionist. She was just checking you'd found me.' She paid the checkout lady and was pleased when Jake took over wheeling the grocery-filled trolley. 'Over there.' She pointed to the silver Mercedes.

'Nice wheels.'

She shrugged. 'Not really my kind. It was my husband's car,' she explained. 'It gets me from here to there and that's all that counts at the moment.' They unloaded the shopping…well, Jake unloaded the shopping, glaring harshly at her when she attempted to lift a bag. 'I used to walk most places but now…' she rubbed the heel of her hand over a part of her abdomen, pushing gently on the little foot which was underneath her ribs '…it's kind of impossible.' She took her keys out of her handbag. 'Did you walk or drive here?'

'Drove.'

'OK. Follow me in your car and we'll take this stuff back to the house.'

'Then to the clinic.' He nodded. 'I heard your conversation.' With that, he stalked to the red Jaguar SS-100 which was parked three cars down.

'Oh, my gosh, is that yours?' She waddled over to the vintage car and ran her fingertips lovingly over the rim of the door. The soft top was down which gave her a complete view of the leather upholstered seats and wood-panelled dashboard. 'This will go down a treat here.'

'Why?'

'*Why?*' She gaped at him. 'You're in the heart of car country, my friend. There's a motor museum not too far from here and we've entered the old vintage ambulance the practice owns in the Bay to Birdwood car race which is at the end of September.' She'd continued to walk around the car as she spoke, inspecting and admiring it as she went. 'Wow. This is so nice. Did you restore it yourself?'

Jake had to admit he was slightly taken aback by her attitude. He'd yet to meet a woman who understood cars and the love he had for them. Now it appeared he'd met one—a pregnant one at that.

'Yes.'

'You've done an incredible job. Can I have a look at the engine?' She'd come to stand before him, her blue eyes glazed with such an honest passion that he found himself even more intrigued than before.

'Of course.' He lifted the concertina hood and stood back to watch her.

'Ooh. Twin carburettors. Do you have much trouble balancing them?'

Jake was momentarily taken aback by her knowledge. 'Uh, no, not really.'

'Weslake and Heynes certainly designed a beautiful engine,' she said after peering more closely at it. She sighed with longing. 'I think I should let you know that I *will* be begging a ride or two while you're here.'

'Of course,' he said again. He lowered the hood and when she didn't say anything else, he gestured to her car. 'Can we get going?'

'Oh, sure. OK.'

He watched as she walked back to her car. She had the true pregnant waddle down pat. He shook his head as though to clear it from thoughts of Rebekah Sanderson— *Dr* Rebekah Sanderson, he corrected himself—who he'd discovered didn't look a day over eighteen, was heavily pregnant and had a passion for vintage cars.

Definitely *not* his type, but intriguing all the same. She drove carefully and responsibly, indicating with enough time for him to follow, and eventually she pulled into a driveway—with a double garage—opposite the medical clinic and across the road from the hospital. At least everything was nice and close.

Jake helped her to unpack and soon learnt where things went as he put the groceries away in the quite spacious but tidy kitchen. Rebekah poured herself a glass of water and slumped down into a chair at the kitchen table.

'Ah. That's nice and cool.' She shifted slightly, rubbing her stomach. 'I could just curl up and sleep for a few hours.' She closed her eyes and tilted her head back, exposing a long expanse of neck. Jake swallowed, his gaze drawn to it. It looked soft and smooth and extremely kissable.

He forced himself to look away and cleared his throat. 'When are you due?'

'Twenty-seven days and counting—*if* the baby comes on time.'

'That soon!' He glanced at her.

'Yes. I'm thirty-six weeks.'

'Sorry. You caught me off guard. I had no idea you were due that soon.'

She opened her eyes. 'Why do you think you're here? Don't I look huge?' She pulled her maternity top around her stomach. 'I'm enormous and getting bigger every day.' Rebekah lovingly patted her baby. 'But I don't mind. So long as I have a healthy baby, that's all that matters.'

'Good philosophy.' Jake paused. 'How old are you?'

'Twenty-eight but I feel a lot older at the moment.'

'You look about eighteen.'

She smiled at his softened tone. Ever since they'd met, his tone had been gruff, almost bordering on impatience. 'I guess the pigtails don't help.'

'No.' He leaned back against the bench, their gazes holding for a second. It stunned him…no, it downright amazed him that he was leaning there, thinking about kissing this woman! This woman who he'd not only just met but who was pregnant with another man's child! He dragged air into his lungs, trying to recover, and pushed away from the bench. 'Clinic,' he stated gruffly, and headed back the way they'd come.

'I was going to…' she lowered her voice as he disappeared completely from view '…give you a tour of the house,' she finished lamely. She sat there for another few moments, gathering up the energy to move. 'Come on, baby.' She stood and followed Jake out. 'Let's finish this day so both you and I can get some rest—and I *mean* rest. When Mummy lies down, that is *not* the time for you to start aerobics. Understand?'

'Pardon?' Jake looked at her.

Rebekah glanced up, not realising he was standing by the back door. 'Lecturing my child.' She shrugged. 'Thought I'd get a head start—especially while it can't talk back.' They walked across the road to the clinic. 'So, as I said before, we weren't expecting you until this evening. Obviously your plans changed.'

'I caught an earlier flight, picked up my car from the rail-yard in Adelaide and drove up here.'

'It's a nice drive. Only two hours from Adelaide city so that's not too bad. Here we are.' She opened the door and watched as Nicole, the clinic's receptionist, turned dreamy-eyed and sighed at seeing Jake.

'Hi, handsome. Good to see you back,' Nicole flirted.

'Any patients for me this afternoon?' Rebekah asked, trying to shift the receptionist's gaze from Jake to herself.

Nicole snapped out of it. 'Just two.'

'How many does Gillian have?'

'She told me not to tell you. Just see your two patients, do your ward round and go home to rest. You know that's what you want to do, Becky.'

She sighed. 'I guess. When's my first patient?'

'Five minutes.'

'Good.' She walked down the small corridor into her consulting room, pleased that Jake had followed. 'Did you meet Gillian when you came in earlier? She's my partner.'

'No.'

'OK. Then I guess you haven't been shown around so I'll do that once I'm finished with the patients. You may as well sit in because no doubt Gillian's going to be insisting you take my measly load completely from my shoulders.'

'I'd agree.'

'Why? You don't even know me.'

'I know you've been through a rough time.'

'Meaning?' she asked cautiously.

'Meaning the other doctor who used to work here died eight months ago. That can't have been easy to deal with.'

'No.' Rebekah was brisk. 'No, it wasn't.'

Jake was curious at the change in her attitude. She'd changed from being bubbly and friendly to putting up a wall but, then, perhaps he shouldn't blame her. One of the doctors in her practice—Guy von Appen—had died. In country and rural practices, you got to know each other *very* well, more so than working in a busy hospital. 'You do know I'm here to finish up the research Guy was doing for me, don't you?'

'Yes. You mentioned that was the primary reason you'd applied for the job.'

'Yes. I needed that data and a break, you needed another GP, although I confess I had no idea it was because you were pregnant.' He indicated her stomach.

'Jake…I wonder if you can tell me why Guy had to go to Sydney so often?' A frown creased her forehead. 'I mean, what was it about the research project that he needed to do in Sydney rather than here?'

'Pardon?' Jake shook his head. 'I'm not sure I understand.'

Rebekah's frown increased. 'What was Guy's part in the research project?'

'He was looking into a few rural cases of pregnant women, who perhaps drank too much alcohol, to see if their unborn babies had FAS—that's foetal alcohol syndrome—'

'I know.'

'Yes, well, some doctors are still quite unaware it exists, hence the research. I needed someone, for the purpose of the research project, to discover and assess any cases in a rural area. Guy volunteered.'

'And that's why you needed to meet him monthly?'

'Monthly? No. He was required to attend a few meetings now and then as well as provide a three-monthly report which could simply be emailed to me.'

'And that's it?' Her tone was hard, almost as though she'd been expecting him to say something along those lines.

'Yes. The last I heard, he had written up some notes but hadn't collated the data.'

'Which is what you've come here to do,' she finished for him. 'So when he came to Sydney, you two often got together?'

'No. Where on earth did you get that idea?' Jake watched as her blue eyes darkened slightly and it was then he noticed her breathing had increased.

'Exactly how well did you know him?'

'What's with all the ques—?'

She slapped a hand down onto her desk in frustration. 'Just answer it…please,' she said between gritted teeth.

'We were professional colleagues…acquaintances at best. We went out a few times when he came to Sydney. Seemed like a nice person.'

Rebekah nodded and met his gaze. 'Always with a different woman?'

Jake started feeling uncomfortable at her words. 'Uh…yes, as a matter of fact. Why? Were you two… involved?' His gaze strayed to her stomach.

'You could say that. We were married for five years.'

Jake felt his jaw drop in surprise before he quickly re-

covered and cleared his throat. 'I had…no idea. Uh…he
never mentioned that he was married.'

She closed her eyes and shook her head. 'Typical.'

'So…the baby?'

'It's his.'

He raked his hand through his hair and exhaled harshly.
What a rotten blow for her. 'Did you know…about the
others, I mean?'

'Not until after his death.' The words were spoken with
a semblance of calm and he realised she was trying to control her blood pressure from exploding. He knew all too
well what that was like. 'I've discovered a lot of things
about the man I was married to in the last eight months,
the main one being that he was never faithful to me during
the entire time of our marriage.'

'I had no idea.'

'Why should you?' Rebekah shook her head. 'Men.'

'Tarring us all with the same brush?'

'Yes. You got a problem with that?'

'I think it's a little judgmental.'

'I feel I have the right, given what I've been through.'

'Fair enough,' he conceded. Jake quickly reminded himself that he was only here to do a job. A job, with a lot
less stress than he was used to, for six months before he
returned to Sydney. What Rebekah Sanderson did with her
life was up to her and if that was to carry a grudge against
his gender, then that was entirely up to her.

'So…anyway, back to business. Next week, you'll be
taking over my almost non-existent patient list as well as
doing house calls with me. Once the baby's born, depending on how things go, we'll split the list between us, although chances are I'd still have to come with you as everyone will insist on seeing the baby. We'll just play it
by ear.'

She was brisk and efficient and in professional mode. The intercom on her desk buzzed. 'Leo's here,' Nicole said.

'Send him in,' Rebekah replied. 'Leo is a seventy-nine-year-old man who has bone cancer. He lives on his own and gets quite lonely sometimes. He sees an oncologist who comes to Angaston hospital—which is our sister hospital—once a month. We manage his pain medication and anything else he needs, while keeping in constant contact with the oncologist. Usual sort of thing.'

While she was speaking, Jake moved his chair off to the side so he wouldn't be in the patient's way. Rebekah went to stand when she saw Leo approaching but he waved her down.

'Don't get up, girl. Stay off yer feet.'

'Leo, I'd like to introduce Dr Jake Carson. He'll be filling in for me while I'm on maternity leave.'

She watched as Leo and Jake shook hands. 'Well, it's good to have yer with us, Doc.' Rebekah had watched the exchange, noting that Jake seemed a little…standoffish with the elderly man. Leo sighed once he was comfortable in the chair and Rebekah returned her attention to him.

'So how have things been going?'

'Not too bad, deary. Not too bad. Old Leo's got more life in him than anyone expected.'

Rebekah smiled. 'I'm glad to hear it. I have a letter here from your oncologist saying that he's very happy with the way you've been responding to treatment, so that's good news. Now, how are your pain levels?'

'Not too bad,' he said again.

'Tell me the truth, Leo. We've been through this before.'

'I just don't like takin' the tablets with morphine in them. There's so many horrible stories about morphine and people becoming addicted.'

'You don't need to worry about that, Leo. We'll keep

things under control. *You* need it, Leo. The pain will be too much for you to cope with otherwise.'

Rebekah reached her hand across the desk and he instantly put his old, weather-beaten one into it. 'Trust me on this. This is why you come here. To make sure your dosages are the right amount, to help relieve you from the constant pain you'd be in without them. You've felt it, you've experienced it and I, for one, don't want you to live like that.'

She'd spoken softly and sincerely and Jake thought the touch of gentle tears shimmering in her eyes were perfect. Leo wouldn't be able to resist her now.

'OK, young Becky, but only because it means so much to ya.' Leo squeezed her hand before letting go. Rebekah smiled at him and nodded before taking in a deep breath. She pulled a tissue from the box on her desk.

'See what you've done to me, Leo.' Although her words were mildly chastising, her smile belied the severity of them. She blew her nose and threw the tissue into the bin. She didn't miss, Jake noticed.

She hefted herself out of the chair and washed her hands. 'Now, while I'm up, is there anything such as bruising or soreness which you'd like me to have a look at?' That prompted Leo to tell her everything that was troubling him. Jake watched as she dealt with everything in a calm and orderly manner and when it was time for Leo to leave she slipped her arm through his and walked him out to the waiting room.

She returned a few minutes later and eased herself back into the chair again.

'That was quite a performance,' he remarked, deciding to test her a little. He'd found it a good way to get a feel for the people he'd be working with.

Rebekah frowned. 'Performance?'

'To get Leo to bend to your will.'

She looked at him as though he'd grown another head. 'Bend to my will? What on earth are you talking about?'

Jake stood and walked around her room, looking at things on the shelves, books, landscape paintings, framed qualifications. She'd been completely genuine with her patient. The tears, the hand squeezes—all of it genuine concern and he was pleased to discover it.

'You think I was being fake to get him to take his medicine? Are you out of your mind?' She shook her head, appalled. There was no way she was leaving her patients in Jake Carson's care if *that* was his attitude. 'I don't know how you practise medicine in Sydney but here in South Australia we're honest with our patients. I've known Leo since I moved here. In fact, he was one of the first people to befriend me. I was the one to break the news to him about his cancer, the one to recommend an oncologist and the one who will be seeing him through this traumatic and emotionally draining time.' She paused but only to drag in another breath before starting again.

'If it didn't take so much effort for me to get out of this chair, I'd…I'd…'

'You'd what?' he challenged.

She glared at him for a moment. 'Escort you out of my clinic, across the road to your car and tell you to drive back to where you came from.'

'And because you *can't* get out of that chair?' He raised his eyebrows. 'Face facts, Dr Sanderson. You need me. I know you've been trying to secure a locum for the past six months at least and I was the first and only nibble you'd had.'

She wanted to refute his statement. To tell him it wasn't true, that they'd had hundreds of applicants all begging for the chance at a six-month contract in the wine district of Tanunda…but she couldn't. He was right.

'That may be true but it certainly has nothing to do with this practice. This is a good medical practice and one which is thriving. The lack of general practitioners in rural and country areas isn't only relevant to South Australia, Dr Carson, but to the rest of Australia as well. Yes, you were our only applicant and your credentials are indeed impressive—' she still prided herself on giving credit where credit was due '—but if you think I run my practice like some two-bit sideshow in order to get my patients to…how did you so eloquently put it…? "bend to my will" then you are sadly mistaken. I don't care if no one else applies for this job, we don't need you here.'

He looked pointedly at her pregnant stomach. 'Really. And the contract I've signed? If you kick me out now, you'll be in breach.'

'My attorney will take care of it.'

'I sincerely hope, for your sake, that it is the *only* breach you encounter.'

She knew he was referring to the baby and it stopped her. 'Why would you care?'

'Because I'm a trained paediatrician. Breech births are extremely difficult, especially for first-time mothers, which I assume you are?'

'Yes. You surprise me, though. Do you care *because* you're trained to or did you train because you *care*?'

Jake walked over and leaned nonchalantly against the edge of her desk, crossed his feet at the ankles and folded his arms across his chest. She shifted back in her chair because he was way closer than she would have liked. Not in a threatening fashion but in a she-was-becoming-very-aware-of-him fashion. He breathed in deeply, his gaze piercing hers. His scent, an expensive one from a bottle, subtly wove its way about her and she reluctantly admitted that she liked it.

'I apologise, Dr Sanderson, if I read your situation with Leo incorrectly. I have witnessed other doctors...' he paused momentarily, thinking of his own partner, '...manipulate their patients emotionally in order for them to accept what's best for them.'

'It's disgusting.'

'In some cases, yes. In others, unfortunately, it's called for.'

She thought about that for a moment and realised he had a point.

'So do I pack my bags?'

Rebekah sighed heavily and rubbed her stomach. 'No. The truth is that we *do* need you but rest assured that Gillian and I *can* and *will* survive without your help if we have to.'

'I understand.' He shifted away from her desk and sat down. 'Now, while we're waiting for your next patient, why don't you tell me about the two hospitals?'

'You should have read about it in the information we sent but it doesn't hurt to reiterate things now you're here.' She launched into her spiel about the district and the merging of Angaston and Tanunda hospitals. 'Tanunda handles the maternity side of things and Angaston—which is twenty minutes away—handles the surgical side. We have a large variety of specialists who come from Adelaide on a regular basis to hold clinics here. If people need elective surgery, then they usually go to Adelaide but we're well equipped to do any emergency surgery.'

'Who does that?'

'I hold a diploma in obstetrics and both Gillian and I hold diplomas in general surgery but again, Gillian's been picking up the slack for me.' The intercom on her desk buzzed, making her jump.

'Scare you again?' Nicole laughed, after Rebekah had answered.

'Yes.'

'Susan's here with Chandra.'

'Thanks. Send them in.' Moments later, a young mother came through with her two-and-a-half-year-old. Once again, Rebekah introduced Jake, explaining who he was and why he was there. Chandra eyed him shyly, hiding her face in her mother's lap. 'What seems to be the problem?'

'She's all snuffly and her glands feel a little swollen around her throat.'

'Have you tried giving her medicine to dry out her nose or nose drops?'

'Yesterday but it hasn't made any difference.'

'Temperature?'

'A slight one last night but the paracetamol did the trick.'

'OK. Come here, Chandra.' Rebekah beckoned her around. 'Would you like to come and say hello to the baby?'

'She was talking about your baby the other day,' Susan put in.

'Were you?'

'Yes.' Chandra came around the desk and placed her hand on Rebekah's stomach. 'Baby.'

'That's right, sweetie. The baby's in there.' Rebekah placed her hand over the tiny one and moved it up a little. 'Feel that? That bump is the baby's foot. Oomph! Did you feel that?' Rebekah smiled. 'Cheeky baby just kicked me.'

Chandra laughed. Rebekah felt the little girl's glands before picking up her torch and tongue depressor. She explained to her patient what she was going to do and showed her how the torch worked. 'Now, say, "Ah".' Chandra obliged. 'Throat looks a little red. I'll just listen to her chest to make sure she's breathing well.' She picked up her stethoscope. 'Remember this?'

Chandra replied by lifting up her dress to reveal her tummy. Rebekah laughed. 'Good girl.' She listened to the front and then the back, noticing there were a few little red dots on Chandra's skin. 'Thank you, sweetie. Her lungs are fine.' She unhooked the stethoscope from her ears and placed it on her desk. 'Just let me have a closer look at your tummy and your back again.'

'What is it?' Susan asked.

'Chickenpox, but as we have our very own paediatrician here, let's get a second opinion.' Now that Rebekah was no longer interested in Chandra's tummy, the little girl dropped her dress, ran back to her mother and looked shyly at Jake once more.

'Hi.' He smiled. His entire face changed, becoming soft where Rebekah had thought it harsh. He looked even more handsome and approachable. It was a powerful smile and was definitely working on Chandra…as well as Rebekah!

'I'm Jake. What's your name?' He held out his hand to the little girl, who quickly looked at her mother for approval. Susan nodded and the next thing they knew, Chandra had hurtled herself into his arms. He laughed in surprise and scooped the little girl up.

Rebekah felt her jaw go slack but couldn't help it. First he'd smiled, then he'd laughed and it was doing crazy things to her equilibrium. Chandra had her chubby little arms about his neck, her head resting trustingly on his shoulder. Rebekah had always considered children a good judge of character and she was amazed the way the toddler was responding to him. If he was like this with all the children he looked after, he'd certainly chosen the right sub-speciality.

'Let's have a look at your tummy.' Chandra proudly lifted her dress for him and he gave her a little tickle. She giggled delightedly and after he'd done the same to her back, he put her back on the floor. 'Perfect diagnosis. Definitely chickenpox.'

Rebekah was secretly delighted with his praise but schooled her features and focused her attention on Susan who now looked rather worried.

'She'll be fine but she has to stay home for at least the next week or so. No playgroup, no going out to the shops or playing with friends.' Rebekah explained more about the virus and handed Susan a fact sheet which contained the relevant information.

'Pinetar liquid, the oil-based one, is great for helping the itching. You can get it at the pharmacy and you put a bit in the bath. Stinks to high heaven but is very effective.'

'What about me? Can I catch it?'

'Did you have chickenpox as a child?'

'Yes, but I'd heard you can get shingles as an adult.'

'Not from chickenpox. You can catch chickenpox from shingles but not the other way around. Shingles—herpes zoster—comes from the chickenpox virus—varicella-zoster. It's a reactivation of the virus which lies dormant, often for years, in the sensory nerve ganglia which is near the spinal cord. Shingles usually happens when a person is run down or severely stressed so in this instance, with Chandra having chickenpox, if you and Vic have had it, then you'll both be fine. Have a read of the fact sheet, speak to the pharmacist and if you have any other questions then give either myself or Gillian a call.'

'OK. Thanks, Becky. You take it easy now.' Susan took Chandra's hand. 'Come on, honey, it's time to go. Say goodbye to Dr Becky.'

'Bye-bye,' the little girl waved, then she turned to Jake and blew him a kiss. He smiled and waved back.

'Well...you're certainly a dark horse,' Rebekah said once they were alone again.

'I presume you're going to explain that statement.'

She placed her elbows on her desk and propped her chin up in her hands. 'You're like a Dr Jekyll and Mr Hyde. As soon as Chandra touched you, you became human.'

He merely raised an eyebrow. 'Have *you* had chicken-pox?'

'Yes, so the baby and I should be just fine but thank you for asking.' Rebekah groaned in pain and shoved the chair away from the desk, placing a hand on her stomach. Jake was up out of his chair and by her side instantly.

'Problem?'

'Ugh. No. I swear this kid is going to be a footballer.' She rubbed her stomach again and when the baby responded, without thinking she reached for Jake's hand and pressed it to her stomach. 'See? Feel that? How strong was that?'

When he didn't answer, she looked up. Their gazes locked and the atmosphere around them seemed to zing with newly charged electrons. Even deep inside her, Rebekah felt them explode and she sucked in a ragged breath.

Jake was stunned! Not by the feel of her baby kicking but by the senses which had travelled up his arm and ripped through his body. He was attracted to this woman! The idea jolted him completely. He didn't even *like* her all that much and yet the desire to bend down and press his lips to hers was...overwhelming. It was the second time since they'd met that he'd been tempted to kiss her. Who *was* she?

It took a few moments for him to realise she'd released her hold on his wrist. Still he left his hand on her stomach for a fraction longer before jerking away and stalking from the room.

CHAPTER TWO

JAKE opened his eyes and stared at the ceiling, furious with himself for not being able to sleep. Why couldn't he get Rebekah out of his mind?

He sat up, swung his legs to the floor and slowly looked around the room which was lit by veiled moonlight. The three framed pictures on the wall were of vintage cars. There was a red Australian jarrah desk in the corner with a comfortable chair, which would be perfect for paperwork. The wardrobe had sufficient coat hangers at one end and ample drawer and shelf space at the other. There were also several fluffy bath towels on one of the shelves.

All in all, she'd gone to a great deal of trouble to make him comfortable—and he appreciated it, except for the scented drawer liners which he'd taken out immediately. He stood and walked over to one of the pictures.

What type of woman liked vintage cars? Guy's wife, that's who! He supposed there were a lot of women who had a passion for older cars, but he'd never come across them before. He raked a hand through his hair and paced around the room. He couldn't believe she'd been married to Guy! The news had thrown him so completely, he'd literally been stunned.

His opinion of his energetic colleague had changed considerably. Jake had first met Guy over a year go and although they'd had several business lunches together, as well as a few casual dinners, Guy had never mentioned anything about his life in Tanunda, other than his practice.

'The jerk.' He whispered the words into the dark. How

could he have cheated on her? She was…beautiful, intel-
ligent and she loved vintage cars. Then again, maybe there
was more to their relationship than he knew. Maybe
Rebekah was the possessive, clingy type of woman who
was a nightmare to live with.

He looked around the room again and shook his head.
'Guess you'll find that out soon enough.' He'd had no idea
that they'd be sharing a house. Sure, he'd been told the job
came with accommodation but not *this*.

Jake heard a sound and stopped moving, listening carefully. His breathing was calm but every sense in his body
was on complete alert. There! Another sound. Someone
was in the house. He quickly pulled on his robe, belting it
loosely, and stealthily moved into the hallway, keeping to
the shadows.

Jake peered around the corner into the kitchen, then felt
all tension leave him as he saw Rebekah standing at the
fridge, the door of which was open, peering inside.
'Couldn't sleep?' he asked, walking into the room.

She jumped sky high and spun to face him. 'For heaven's
sake, don't go creeping up on me like that.' She placed one
hand over her heart, the other on the baby, her pulse slowly
returning to normal. She grinned at him and flicked her
loose hair over her shoulder. 'Although if I go overdue I
could scare me into labour.' She returned her attention to
the fridge and pulled out the pickles and bananas. She was
dressed in an oversized nightshirt, her robe open and hanging down her back, and pink fluffy slippers on her feet.

'Baby won't settle,' she offered by way of explanation
as she put the food onto the table. 'Would you mind getting
me the chocolate spread down from that cupboard, please?'
She pointed the direction before turning back to the fridge.
'Want anything?' she asked, taking out a large bottle of
ginger beer.

'No.' He put the chocolate spread on the table. Her hair was cascading smoothly over her shoulder and the urge to run his fingers through it surprised him.

'Keep me company.' She put a plate and knife on the table and eased herself down. 'Whew. I tell you, just getting up and down now is such an effort. I'll be glad when this is all over.'

'You'll still have to get up and down to the baby,' he pointed out as he sat.

'Sure but at least I won't be lugging him or her around with me twenty-four seven. The baby can sleep in the bassinet and I can enjoy having my body back to myself.'

'Except for feeding. You are going to breast-feed, I presume.' His gaze dropped to the area in question and she felt a burning heat rip through her.

Rebekah looked away, confused and amazed at her body's response. 'Yes.' She cleared her throat. 'Yes, I am.' It was ridiculous. She was a doctor and so was he. Why was she feeling so self-conscious all of a sudden? She would have liked to have pulled her dressing-gown over her chest but the simple fact was that it didn't fit around her middle any more. Instead, she tugged on her nightshirt and reached for a pickle.

'Are you sure you don't want a pickle? Come on,' she continued, not waiting for an answer. 'Smeared with chocolate spread, they're even yummier.' She spread the chocolate as she spoke and held one out to him, expecting him to turn his nose up in disgust. Instead, the rich sound of his laughter filled the kitchen as he politely refused.

'I'm sure they're an acquired taste.'

Rebekah smiled back, pleased she'd cracked his defences. After he'd stalked out of her consulting room, she'd sat there confused. She hadn't been sure where he'd gone but as she'd had to go over to the hospital, she'd waddled

across and had found him deep in discussion with Monica,
the clinical nurse consultant.

Together the three of them had done a round of the hospital, with Monica introducing Jake to the rest of the staff.
In the end, Rebekah had wondered why she'd even bothered! Throughout all the time she'd spent with him so far,
he'd been polite and standoffish…and now she'd not only
got him to smile but laugh as well.

'I was beginning to wonder whether there was a human
being beneath that professional façade.'

The smile instantly vanished and she knew she'd said
the wrong thing.

'What I mean is…that I know it can be hard, you know,
starting a new job and everything and it can sometimes get
a bit overwhelming. It's nice to see you relaxing a little.'

Jake nodded and stood. 'I'll leave you to snack in peace.'

'Hey.' Rebekah went to heave herself out of the chair
but he held up his hand, stopping her.

'No. Stay where you are. You're obviously comfortable.'

'Stay and talk to me,' she said as he walked in the direction of his room. 'Jake, I'm sorry if my words seemed
offensive. I didn't mean it that way.'

'It's fine.' He turned and faced her but by then she'd
managed to stand. 'I wasn't offended so you can put your
mind at ease.'

'Then what is it? Don't you like having friendships with
people you work with?'

Jake shrugged. He was uncomfortable around her. Not
because she was annoying or irritating but because he
couldn't help the unwanted attraction he felt.

'You've come straight from a large Sydney hospital,
haven't you?'

'Correct.'

'People there always keep their distance. If they get involved with someone they work with on a personal level someone might actually find out who they are deep down inside.'

If he'd been uncomfortable before, it was nothing compared to now and it was mainly because she'd hit the nail right on the head. In a matter of hours of their first meeting, Rebekah Sanderson had seen right through to the heart of him and it completely unnerved him.

'I'm going to go now.'

She saw it. The mask had come down in place but for a brief second, when he'd laughed, she'd seen the *real* him. Now that man had disappeared completely and the cool, calm professional was back in place.

'Jake.' She took a few steps forward and reached out a hand to him. He took a step away. 'I'm sorry if I've probed or pried but I just…thought…we could be friends.' She shrugged.

'Look, Dr Sanderson, all I want for the next six months is to get out of bed, do my job, collate the research information and spend my evenings in peace.'

She stared at him for a long moment before nodding. 'OK. If that's the way you want it, that's fine.' There was no anger in her tone, no girlish outrage, but he thought he detected a hint of pity which was the last thing he wanted. 'But, please, do you think you could call me Rebekah? Becky is fine, too, but…' She smiled tiredly at him. 'Dr Sanderson? That's bound to raise a few eyebrows and give people the impression you don't like me.' She walked back to the chair and sat. 'And we all know that's just not true,' she teased.

Jake was tempted to smile again. She had an ease and natural friendliness he'd never come across before. Instead he acknowledged her words. 'OK. Goodnight…Rebekah.' With that, he turned and walked out the kitchen.

Rebekah slumped forward and sighed heavily. 'Boy, are the next six months going to be fun,' she told her stomach as she reached for another pickle.

When she woke on Saturday morning, Rebekah felt as though she'd been put through the wringer. She turned on her side, swung her legs over the edge of the bed and slowly pushed herself upright, keeping her eyes closed in an effort to stop the spinning.

Gradually opening her eyes, she tried to focus but it was no good and a wave of nausea hit with force. She clamped a hand over her mouth and rushed to her bathroom. Once her early morning dash was over, she showered and dressed, beginning to feel much better even though she was already exhausted.

'No one said the last trimester was easy,' she mumbled as she shuffled into the kitchen.

'Feeling better?'

She stopped. Jake was sitting at the kitchen table dressed in a pair of casual trousers and a navy, cotton shirt and eating a stack of pancakes drowned in maple syrup. She sniffed appreciatively and smiled as she walked over to the stove.

'Yes, thank you. I guess baby didn't want the pickles and chocolate spread after all. These, however, smell delicious.' She peered at the pancake batter in the jug. 'So does this mean you know how to cook?'

'It does. Please, help yourself.'

Rebekah did just that and soon was sitting down with one pancake, smothered in maple syrup. 'Mmm. These are heavenly.'

By now, Jake had finished his breakfast and was stacking the dishwasher. 'Are you usually sick in the morning?'

'No. Not really. I mean it depends on what I've snacked on around three o'clock in the morning.'

'That's your usual routine?'

'At the moment but some advice I was given regarding children is that just when you think you've got them into a routine, they change it. So I'm not holding out because Junior here changes his or her mind almost as much as I do.'

'Have you spoken to your obstetrician about your morning sickness?'

'Yes. He's happy with the way things are. Besides, my blood pressure is fine, my ankles aren't swollen and so far, apart from the odd food disagreeing with Junior, I've had quite an uneventful pregnancy.'

'If you don't mind my asking...' His tone was gentle as he set the coffee-machine in motion before sitting back down. 'When did you find out you were pregnant?'

'Two weeks after Guy died.' She leaned back and rubbed a hand over her stomach. 'Did you enjoy that, my sweetheart, because mummy certainly did.'

'So, this was where the two of you lived?'

'Yes.'

'It doesn't...bother you? Doing the renovations, I mean.'

'No. Quite cathartic, really. Smashing down walls and remodelling the house mirrors how I feel about my own life. I've smashed down a lot of personal walls, personal hurts which Guy's betrayals have inflicted.' She lovingly rubbed her stomach. 'Now *I'm* remodelling.' She looked up at him. 'This house really is too big for just me and the baby but as it doesn't *really* belong to me, I thought I'd pass the time by putting in a few extra walls and making the end you're in into a little guest-unit type thing.'

'I'm sorry.' He frowned, now wishing he hadn't asked

in the first place. 'Did you say the house *doesn't* belong to you?'

'Correct. It's in trust, for the baby. Guy owned it as well as a part-share in the family vineyard not far from here. None of the family are there now. His parents moved to France after Guy's funeral and left the property in the hands of very good caretakers so when Junior here is twenty-one years old, he—or she—gets to inherit the lot.'

Her words had been said matter-of-factly. It intrigued Jake more than he wanted. 'You said you were married for five years.'

'Yes, except it appears that *my* version of marriage and *Guy's* version of marriage were two completely different things.'

'So it would seem.'

Rebekah sighed. 'That was my old life. I now have a new one I need to concentrate on.' She smiled brightly—a little too brightly, he thought as she levered herself up. 'Thanks so much for breakfast. Gillian's doing Saturday morning clinic so we don't need to bother with that although you will be rostered on once a fortnight.'

'I know.' He'd read his job description quite thoroughly.

'OK, then. Well, how about I slip some shoes on and we'll head off to Angaston hospital so you can meet everyone there?'

'Good.'

When Rebekah returned, she'd tied her hair back into a ponytail and added a scarf. 'Mind if we take your car?' She batted her eyelashes at him pleadingly and hoped her mouth had formed a pout.

He chuckled and she relished the sound, sorry when he quickly covered it over with a cough. 'You can't wait to have a ride, can you?' Even though he'd pulled himself into line, the twinkle was still in his eyes.

'Well, I did warn you.' He held the door open for her and she headed outside into the April sunshine. 'There'll be more traffic on the road today, being a weekend and all.'

'Tourists?'

'In droves but it's great for the area.'

'Bad for the doctors?'

'No. We're only called in to the hospital when necessary. Poor Gillian's been covering the past few weekends even though I told her it was no trouble for me to do one, but she's like a mother to me and clucks over me like an expectant grandmother.' Rebekah sank down into the comfortable, upholstered leather. 'Nice,' she sighed. 'Oh, this is *very* nice.' She waited until he was seated. 'How much of the internal restoring did you do yourself?'

'I didn't do the seats or the dash but I certainly banged out a lot of dints and hunted through old junk yards until I found just the things I needed. The engine was my speciality. I know it intimately.'

Rebekah nodded. 'That's how I was with the ambulance. It lives at the motor museum where it's lovingly cared for but they allow me visitation rights.' She laughed. 'The engine purrs with perfection. I'm very proud of it.'

As Jake started the car and reversed out of her driveway he gave her a quizzical look. 'You restored the engine?'

'Sure did.'

'You're the first woman I've ever heard enthuse to the point of obsession over a car.'

'What do you mean, to the *point* of obsession? I *am* obsessed. Just as you are.' She laughed and closed her eyes, enjoying the feel of the wind on her face.

'How did you get into it? Older brothers who did up cars?'

Rebekah didn't move. Just kept her face turned to the wind and her eyes closed. 'No,' she said eventually.

Realising she didn't want to talk about it, he took the hint. 'How does tourism impact the hospitals and clinics?'

She lifted her head and glanced across at him before slipping on a pair of sunglasses. 'This is wine country. The famous Barossa Valley. Tanunda, Nuriootpa, Angaston—they're all part of the most gorgeous countryside in Australia. The majority of tourists come for the wine tasting. There's a train that does regular trips up and back so at least they don't bring their cars and drive back to Adelaide drunk but a lot of tourists also come for the scenery. The chateaux around here are old and have a lot of history to tell.' She paused. 'Turn right at the end of the street.

'But with regard to the patients, we have the odd emergency—burst appendix, perforated ulcers, that sort of thing. Food poisoning pops up every now and then. Coughs, colds, things people don't think to take care of during the week because they're so busy working then when they come up here for a quick weekend break, their bodies collapse from exhaustion and they easily pick up a bug or virus.

'We've had plenty of broken limbs, through various means. One teenage boy came in with a Colles' fracture.' Rebekah smoothed her fingers over her wrist. 'He'd fractured it by doing a one-handed cartwheel in the grounds of one of the chateaux. We do have a few more car accidents with those who *are* stupid enough to drink and drive but we haven't had anything major for years. Go left at the T-junction.'

She sighed wistfully. 'We're just a sleepy little area nestled amongst vines and trees.' She pointed to the trees which were losing their leaves, their lovely autumn reds, greens and yellows blurring into a beautiful mass of colours. 'Guess it's vastly different from what you're used to.'

'Yes. Now, tell me, what's with the scarecrows?' He pointed to a scarecrow dressed as a ballet dancer at the front of a house. 'Look, there's some more.' Three scarecrows dressed as angels were outside an old church.

'It's something the locals do for the Barossa Vintage Festival. There's a competition going for the best scarecrow and you can vote at the information centre. It's a lot of fun. There's a scarecrow dressed as a doctor outside Angaston hospital. Cricketers in a vineyard, a scarecrow fishing by the river—that's my favourite.'

'So it's just for fun?'

'Yes. At Christmas-time, everyone puts red or green bows on the front of their houses and the trees and shops in the main street also have bows on. It looks amazing.'

'A real…welcoming atmosphere.'

'Yes. The people coming for the festival love it and we all love being a part of it.' She continued to gave him directions but neither of them spoke for a few minutes. When they pulled into the hospital car park, Rebekah turned to look at him. 'Jake?'

'Hmm?'

'I'm sorry if I've been overly nosy. What you said earlier today—that you just want to do your job and that's it—well, I want you to know that I respect that. We all have our own private thoughts and we're entitled to keep them private if we so choose. I do respect that and I don't want you to think that I was deliberately pushing because I wasn't. I was just trying…to be…friends. Not the live-in-your-pocket-and-tell-you-everything-type friend but just something more than professional acquaintances who happen to share a house. I mean, you obviously heard me vomiting this morning so as far as I'm concerned that kind of raises the level of intimacy, and it's one that professional acquaintances usually don't share.'

Jake undid his seat belt and turned slightly to face her. 'The level of our relationship will be different from being just colleagues, as you've said. I can see that and while we're being honest here, I'd like you to know that I don't have a lot of experience in that area. I haven't lived with anyone since I left home so if I'm a little…rough around the edges, sometimes, I hope you'll excuse me.'

Her smile was genuine and he felt its full force. He didn't want to be moved by her. It was one of the reasons he not only *wanted* to keep his distance but seemed to *need* it as well. Rebekah Sanderson was…an enigma and one he didn't want to discover—or so he told himself.

'I'll certainly try,' she replied. 'So now that I know how you behave around your peers, tell me how you are with the patients because really, when all is said and done, that's what's going to count the most.'

Jake smiled sardonically. 'Why don't we go inside and you can grade me?' He opened his door and climbed from the car before walking around to help her out. He took both her hands in his and after she'd swung her legs around, she stood. Without letting go of his hands, she looked deeply into his eyes.

'Are you teasing me?' she asked softly, trying desperately hard to ignore the heat radiating from him.

Jake was mesmerised by the light blue flecks which surrounded her pupils and felt as though he was getting a glimpse into her soul. He jerked back, the moment broken before he shoved his hands into his pockets. 'Teasing you?' He thought about it. 'Feels like it…but as I haven't teased anyone for about…let me think…ten years, I've forgotten what it's like.'

Rebekah's smile was as bright as the sun in the sky. 'I'll let you in on a secret,' she whispered, leaning in a little closer. 'You're doing a good job.' She straightened before she could breathe in any more of his mesmerising scent, which in turn caused her head to go even more fuzzy than it already was, and led the way into Angaston hospital.

Jake watched as she conversed easily with staff and patients. She greeted them all like old friends and introduced him to everyone they came across, even the domestic staff which was something he found a little strange. In a large hospital you never had time to get to know *everyone* on staff yet here it appeared Rebekah not only knew everyone, she knew what was going on in their lives—and they in hers. He shuddered. The intimacies of small, rural towns were not for him.

'Was I right?' she asked Clive, one of the male cleaners, who was swinging a polisher over the floors. They were on their way out after doing an extremely long ward round while she caught up with everyone.

'As usual. Hetty bought some of that manuka honey, swirled it around her gums and, sure enough, the ulcers started disappearing.'

'I'm glad.'

He stopped, turned the polisher off and pressed his hand to her stomach. 'How's our baby doing?'

'Just fine.'

'Not long now.'

'No. Not long now.' She smiled, waiting patiently for him to remove his hand before continuing down the corridor of the twenty-six-bed hospital to the front door, calling her goodbyes. 'See you tomorrow,' she said to the CNC.

'Tomorrow!'

Rebekah stopped at the other woman's tone.

'Rebekah Sanderson, you are *not* picking grapes in your condition. Does Gillian know?'

'That I'm planning to go like I do every year? Yes.'

'This year's a little different, Becky. You're in no condition to pick grapes.' Sister waggled a finger at her.

'What if I promise not to overdo it?' she asked hopefully.

Sister relented with a smile. 'Well...we'll have to see.' She placed her hand on the baby. 'I'm positive it's a girl.'

'I guess we'll find out when it's born. See you tomorrow,' she said again, before heading out to Jake's car. He'd started the engine and had pulled out onto the main road before the questioning began.

'Grape picking?'

'Sure. Have you ever done it before?'

He shook his head. 'Can't say that I have. I prefer to drink the wine from a bottle once the entire process has been finished.'

'Leaving it up to the experts?'

'Something like that.'

'Doesn't take an expert to snip off a bunch of grapes. Besides, it can actually be a lot of fun. I think you'll enjoy it.'

'Pardon?'

'I said I think you'll—'

'I heard what you said but why did you say it?'

'Because you're coming.'

'To where?'

'To the vineyard tomorrow.'

'What vineyard?'

'Didn't I tell you? Gillian and her husband have a few acres of vines. Quite small, compared to the large companies around here. Every year we all go and help pick the grapes.'

'They don't have machines?'

'No. At Guy's family's vineyard they do but Gillian's place isn't set up for the machines so we pick by hand.'

'So what does all this grape-picking stuff have to do with me?'

'I volunteered you. All the medical staff—if they're not on duty at the hospitals—get invited to Gillian's house for the day. It's a lot of fun and a good way to catch up with people. Lots of other people come, of course, so you'll be getting to know the locals as well. A good *en masse* introduction for you.'

'Did Guy ever go?'

Rebekah looked down at her hands. 'I managed to drag him there once but it wasn't his…you know…sort of thing.'

'I still find it hard to believe that the two of you were married.'

'I still find it hard to believe he cheated on me.'

'Do you miss him? I mean, regardless of what he did, do you miss him?' It was an important question. Jake didn't realise *how* important it was to him until he'd asked it.

Rebekah thought for a moment and sighed. 'Right now I'd have to say I miss the…security he offered.' She rubbed a hand over her stomach.

'From what you've said, he's more than adequately provided for you and the baby.'

'I'm not talking about material possessions but we didn't…plan this baby and soon I'm going to be a single mother, responsible for the child's upbringing. It scares me senseless.'

'I'm sure he didn't plan to die.'

'No.' Melancholy wrapped itself around her as she leaned back and closed her eyes, hardly feeling the breeze and hardly noticing the smells. 'So, will you come grape picking tomorrow?'

'Yes.' He watched her, with her head tipped back, her eyes closed. 'You're tired,' he stated. 'Let's get you home.'

They lapsed into silence until he pulled the car into her driveway. 'We're here.' He gently placed a hand on her shoulder to wake her but he couldn't. She was out for the count. He climbed from the car, opened the unlocked back door to the house before returning for Rebekah. There was no way he could let her sleep in such an uncomfortable position because it wouldn't do her or the baby any good.

He slowly and carefully helped her from the car but still she didn't wake completely. He placed an arm about her shoulders to help, but when she sagged against him he did the only thing possible—swung her into his arms.

She was surprisingly light and it was then he realised he'd never carried a pregnant woman before. She placed a lethargic arm about his neck and snuggled in.

'Mmm. You smell nice,' she murmured sleepily.

Jake smiled, despite himself, and carried her through to her room. She didn't smell too bad either. As fresh as a rose garden but not in an overpowering way. He placed her gently on the unmade bed, watching as she snuggled into the pillows. 'Thank you.' The words were hardly audible but he appreciated them all the same as he pulled the covers around her.

It was then he realised he couldn't move. He simply stood there, watching her sleep. She still looked about eighteen years old. He shook his head slightly, surprised his heart rate had increased. Her hair had fallen across her face and before he could stop himself he smoothed it back, astounded that his hand wasn't as steady as he would have liked.

She was beautiful, no doubt about that, and not in a conventional way. He'd dated his fair share of debutantes and socialites in the past and all of them had been beautiful but...Rebekah Sanderson...there was something extremely different about her. Something was drawing him in. He wanted to get closer, wanted to know the answers to questions he had no right to ask.

He raked a hand through his hair, exhaling slowly as he tried to control himself. He turned away only to have his gaze rest on a guilded photo frame which held a picture of Rebekah on her wedding day.

So it was true. Ever since she'd told him that she'd been Guy's wife, he'd wanted to dispute the fact. Now here was the proof—in colour. A colleague he'd respected had been cheating on his wife. Unable to stop himself, he crossed to her dresser to examine the picture. Guy smiled at the camera, pressing his cheek to Rebekah's.

She looked happy and he realised even though she'd laughed, teased and smiled since he'd arrived, he hadn't seen her looking happy, as she did in the photo. Had *Guy* made her happy?

As soon as the thought came, Jake pushed it away, telling himself it was none of his business. This woman meant nothing to him on a personal level. Theirs was a working relationship and it would remain that way.

He had a life—a life in Sydney which he would return to in six months' time. Hopefully, by then, the threat of a stress coronary, which was currently hanging over his head, would have settled down and he could get on with his career. Coming here to a rural area had been a strategic move, one designed to help him slow his pace a little. Rebekah Sanderson was not part of the equation.

'Hmm… Jake.' The word was whispered from Rebekah's lips as she sighed and rested a hand possessively on her stomach.

At the breathless sound of his name on her lips, his gut wrenched—in a spasm of delight. This woman was dan-

gerous. She was making him feel things he didn't want to—
couldn't—feel and it was starting to get to him.

He riffled his fingers through his hair again and forced
himself to leave her room…immediately.

CHAPTER THREE

JAKE had heard Rebekah wake during the night and had stayed where he was. Safe, in his room.

There was no way he was going through a repeat of the previous early morning rendezvous where Rebekah had looked amazingly...alluring. It was crazy and he couldn't figure out why he was so attracted to this pregnant woman.

It wasn't as though he hadn't been around pregnant women before either. As a paediatrician, he'd seen his fair share, especially if the baby was diagnosed with a genetic defect before birth. So why? Why was this happening?

Just before six o'clock he gave up any pretence of sleep and headed to his bathroom to shower. Afterwards, he felt more like himself. A man in control. Walking into the kitchen, he was surprised to find Rebekah sitting at the table, eating a bowl of cereal.

'Have you been up all night?' She was dressed in a red knit top with three-quarter-length sleeves. The colour made her hair seem darker than before, and it definitely suited her.

She looked up and smiled as she finished her mouthful. 'No, but it's grape-picking day and we always get an early start.'

'You are *not* picking grapes,' he said with more force than was necessary.

Rebekah laughed. 'Now you're starting to sound like everyone else in this town. I might help out but only with the vines which are at chest height. My brain hasn't completely turned to mush.'

44

'Glad to hear it.' He took a box of cereal from the cup-board.

'You don't need to eat. Breakfast is provided and it's a lavish spread.'

He put the cereal away and looked at her bowl.

'Junior was hungry.' She grinned and carried her bowl to the sink. The black skirt she wore swished around her legs and she adjusted the hem of the red top so it wasn't crinkled over her stomach. 'Coffee's almost done. Want a cup?'

'Yes.'

'Go on.' She reached for two mugs and added sugar to his, having noted the previous day that he had his coffee with one sugar with a few drops of milk. 'Say it, Jake. It'll make you feel better.'

'What?'

'The warning about me not drinking coffee.'

'I obviously don't need to.'

'I know but it'll make you feel better.' She poured her-self half a cup and then added hot water and milk, diluting it. 'After all, you are the expert on birth defects and foetal syndromes.' She made his coffee as she spoke.

'Yes.' He took the cup she held out to him and sipped appreciatively. 'Which means you should listen when I speak.'

'Oh, yes, sir,' she responded immediately, and saluted. The corners of his mouth twitched and she congratulated herself on getting him to smile so early in the day. 'So, does the fact that you're up and ready to shake, rattle and roll mean you're really coming grape picking with me?'

'Someone's got to keep an eye on you.'

'Ha. Trust me, Jake. Everyone there will be keeping an eye on me.'

'Protective of you?'

'You could say that.'

'Why?'

'Because I'm a woman whose husband died less than a year ago and I'm about to give birth.' Her words were slightly clipped. She drank her coffee and put her cup in the sink without looking at him. 'I'll just grab my handbag and then I need to stop off at the clinic to pack my medical bag and then we can go.' When she returned, she was her bright, happy self and they headed outside. 'I won't be a moment,' she said, heading over to the clinic. 'You can wait in the car if you'd prefer.'

Jake walked beside her. 'Expecting some emergencies today?'

She shrugged. 'There's the usual. Cuts, scrapes, mosquito bites.'

'Mosquitoes?'

'Yes. Because the vines are constantly drip-watered, this makes shallow puddles which are an ideal breeding ground for—'

'Mozzies.' They said together.

She packed her bag, going over the check list twice before locking up the clinic and walking back to her house. 'Can we take your car again? It's a dream to drive in.'

'Of course.' He held the door for her before heading around to the driver's seat. 'If you weren't pregnant, I'd even let you have a drive but the seats don't adjust all that well.'

'Never you mind. I'll hold you to that once the baby's born.'

Jake started the engine and followed her directions.

'Go left here and then it's the third driveway on the right. There'll be a sign or something out.' She breathed in deeply. 'Stinks, doesn't it?'

'Yes.'

'But the vines look beautiful. I love the colours. The reds, yellows, oranges and greens all blended together. I love autumn, it's my favourite time of year. Especially here.'

'It is rather pretty. Reminds me of Europe.'

'Does it? I've never been but I do love the...ambience here.'

'But what *is* that smell? It's like...alcohol and...' He sniffed.

'Manure,' she supplied.

'Exactly.' He turned into the driveway and up the winding road.

'The vineyard owners have to save water where they can, so it's recycled into "grey" water. Sometimes this can give off an...interesting aroma but it's worse after the grapes have been crushed.'

'And this is supposed to be fun,' he stated dryly.

Rebekah laughed as Gillian's house came into view. 'Yes, so make sure you enjoy it.'

Why did her laughter mesmerise him like that? It was as though for a second, just a small second in time, she was happy again, like in her wedding picture...even if the smile still didn't make her eyes sparkle as brightly.

The house was surrounded with cars parked at all sorts of angles and Jake managed to find a space not too far from where the festivities were taking place. He came around and helped Rebekah out of the car. The touch of his hand on hers was enough to make her pulse jump into the next gear and start racing with anticipation.

'Thank you.' The words came out on a breathless whisper. She glanced down at the ground and cleared her throat before meeting his gaze once more and smiling shyly up at him. 'I'm not used to playing the damsel in distress but there's no way I can get out of the car without help—at the moment.' She tried to laugh off the feelings he was evoking, telling herself she was silly for even experiencing them in the first place. Look at her, for heaven's sake. What man would find her attractive?

'I don't think you're a damsel in distress.' His eyes were intense with sincerity, his deep voice slightly husky and filled with promise. 'I think you're a radiant mother-to-be.'

Rebekah swallowed, unable to look away. They were standing closer than she'd realised and she could still smell the fresh scent of his shower. She was tempted to throw herself into his arms and press her lips to his. *Very* tempted.

Everything around them became a blur as they continued to focus solely on each other. If he leaned a little closer, he'd be able to brush his lips across hers. Jake lowered his gaze to watch her lips part, her teeth nipping the lower one slightly.

Desire—surprising yet very real—raced through him at an alarming rate and he forced himself to take a step away.

As he closed the car door behind her, Rebekah was thankful for the momentary reprieve as she tried to squash the emotions he was forcing to the surface. She cleared her throat. 'I'd better go find Gillian. Would you mind passing me my bags, please?' Once she had them she walked quickly towards the house. He was surprised at her speed. The only time he'd seen a pregnant woman walk that quickly had been when she'd needed to go to the bathroom! Perhaps that's where Rebekah was headed…or perhaps she wanted to get away from him.

Either way, he was glad there was a growing distance between them. What had he been thinking? 'Just do your job and get back to your life,' he muttered to himself as he followed the direction Rebekah had taken.

'Yoo-hoo! Dr Carson.' He turned at the sound of his name. He was just about to head up the few steps to the front door when Nicole came around the side of the house. 'We're all out the back. Here.' She linked her arm through his. 'I'll show you.'

Jake forced himself to smile. Was this the country hospitality he'd heard of? Coming from the city, he'd never experienced it before and wasn't too happy he had to endure it now. He just wasn't a touchy-feely sort of man—especially with strangers.

'Look who's here,' Nicole chattered as they came around the house to the rear entertaining area where about twenty-five people were gathered. He glanced around, looking for Rebekah, but she wasn't among them.

There were several choruses of 'Hi, there' and 'Hi, Doc' and two elderly women, both with lavender hair, came over.

'Ooh. We've been so excited to meet you, haven't we, Sylvia?'

'Ooh, yes, Margaret. We've been waiting since we heard you had arrived the other day.'

'I'm pleased to meet you,' Jake replied, and held out his hand. Sylvia went first and held his hand for a bit too long.

'Let go. It's my turn,' Margaret growled.

Jake was mildly surprised and tried to smother a smile. The mild scent of roses he'd come to associate with Rebekah teased at his senses and he automatically looked around for her. She was standing just behind him.

'Now, now,' she said. 'Sylvia and Margaret you don't need to fight over him. There's more than enough to share.'

'Ooh, Dr Sanderson.' Sylvia giggled. 'You are funny.' Sylvia placed her hand on Rebekah's stomach. 'How's our baby today?'

'Hungry.'

'Again?' Jake raised his eyebrows. 'You've just finished a bowl of cereal.'

'Oh, shush,' Margaret chastised. 'Leave her alone. You wouldn't know anything about motherhood.'

'Dr Carson is a qualified paediatrician,' Rebekah put in. 'So he would know more than the average man.'

'But he will *never* know what it's like to have a baby inside him so he ought not to pick on you if you're hungry, regardless of when you last ate,' Sylvia added.

'Come along, dear. Sylvia, get her a seat while I get her some food. Dr Willis has outdone herself again this year and has a wide selection to choose from.' Margaret took Rebekah's hand and started pulling her towards the tables of food. 'Now, what does baby feel like?'

Rebekah glanced at Jake before shrugging her shoulders and allowing herself to be led away.

'Now that the Munroe sisters have whisked Becky away, it looks like it's up to me to...show you around,' Nicole purred. Jake forced a smile back into place, wondering how soon he could leave without appearing rude. Surely there would be no shortage of people to give Rebekah a lift home. After all, it wasn't as though they'd come together— as a couple.

Then again, maybe she'd get tired and need to go home to lie down. Then he'd be more than happy to take her. Nicole took him over to meet a few people. He nodded and smiled politely while letting everyone else do the talking.

'I'm so glad you're in that house with her,' one woman said.

'That's right. We were all very worried, especially now she's getting to the end of her pregnancy, so if anything happens, she has you in the house to help her,' said another.

'She needs a man around.'

'A good one. Not like that unfaithful husband of hers.'

'She should have divorced him.'

'Well, she probably would have if he'd lived.'

'If only we'd all known sooner, we could have pro-
tected her.'

'Well we can protect her now and the baby. They'll both
be loved and cared for by all of us. These eggs Benedict
are lovely. I'll have to tell Gillian. Excuse me.'

For the next hour people chatted and gossiped and Jake
ate his food and listened. It was hard not to! He was also
very conscious of exactly where Rebekah was the entire
time and the knowledge bothered him. He told himself it
was a natural, medical reaction. When a woman was so
heavily pregnant, it was his job as a medical professional
to make sure she was all right. He was also aware of Sylvia,
who had confessed to a heart problem, so that proved that
any concern he might feel towards his pregnant colleague
was within reason.

A few bottles of wine had been opened during breakfast
and when he saw Rebekah pouring herself a glass of red,
he excused himself from the conversation and was by her
side like a shot.

'What are you doing?'

'Having a sip of wine.'

'Do you think that's wise?'

'It's only a glass, Jake, and a small one at that.'

'You shouldn't be drinking when you're pregnant.'

She smiled at him. 'I'd hardly call having one glass
"drinking" but I appreciate your concern. Now, I promised
Gillian I'd take it easy so I'm going to sit down and relax.'
With that, she went inside the house, the back door banging
shut in his face.

Two hours later, the grape picking had well and truly
begun. Once he'd been shown what to do, Jake worked
quickly and efficiently, hoping to get out of there sooner.
He was by no means a stranger to hard work but if he had

the choice between picking grapes and something else, he probably would have chosen something else.

'Having fun?'

He glanced up at Rebekah who was standing to the left of him, sipping from a glass of wine. Jake scowled.

'It's the same glass,' she told him defensively. 'It is also the only glass of wine I've had since finding out I was pregnant and I started it over two hours ago.'

Jake placed the last bunch of grapes he'd snipped into the bucket provided and stood to stretch his back.

'Working you too hard?'

'Not at all. This is probably just the kind of thing the doctor recommends when he says he wants people to relax.' He growled the words, a frown on his face.

Rebekah eyed him carefully. 'Are you supposed to be relaxing?'

He mumbled something as he turned back to the grapes.

'Jake?'

'I'm supposed to be unwinding, yes.' He didn't turn to face her.

'Why?'

Jake turned quickly and glared at her. 'Are you ready to go home yet?' The words came out more clipped than he'd intended.

Rebekah merely laughed. 'Had enough, eh? I think you should know, though, that Gillian also puts on a great spread for lunch. If you thought breakfast was good, you ain't seen nothin' yet.'

So it looked as though he was staying. 'I'd say Gillian has the right idea. Inside, preparing food, while the real workers are out here.'

'That almost sounds like sour grapes to me.' She chuckled and he groaned at her corny joke. 'Why don't you come in and have a rest for a while? No one will mind. From what I've heard, you've been filling the buckets faster than anyone else so that should do your ego the world of good.'

'I don't care about my ego,' he said as they started towards the house. 'But I wouldn't mind leaving.'

Rebekah swallowed her disappointment. She had to keep reminding herself that he was from the city. He wasn't used to the slower pace of life and although she hardly knew him, she still thought he could do with slowing down a bit. He appeared to be a classic type A, all work and no play. She took a breath and looked up at him, forcing a smile. 'Don't feel you have to stay on my account. There are plenty of people who can take me home when I'm ready.'

How had she done that? Now he felt like a jerk for wanting to leave and although part of him wanted to continue walking to the car once they'd reached the house, another part—the one his parents had trained to do the right thing and have good manners—knew he should stay.

He looked down into her face and was surprised at the disappointment he saw there. Sure, she was trying to hide it but he saw it, briefly, before her fake smile slid into place. Was she disappointed he was leaving the party…or leaving her? He pushed that thought aside.

'Well, if lunch is as magnificent as you say it is, I'd be a fool to miss it.' Her smile brightened instantly at his words and he felt something unwanted twist in his gut— the unwanted attraction to Rebekah Sanderson.

She linked her arm through his, as though it were the most natural thing in the world, and led him inside. When Nicole had done the same thing earlier, he'd been slightly annoyed but again, good manners had had him politely accepting the unwanted advance. Now, though, when Rebekah did it, he found nothing insinuating in her touch, neither did he see anything in her expressive eyes other than happiness.

He'd made her happy. Happy because he'd agreed to stay. Was it really that simple? As she led him into a comfortable sitting room, he wondered whether any other woman had looked up at him the way Rebekah just had—with simple, untainted happiness.

'So what made you change your mind?' she asked quietly after she'd placed her glass on the coffee-table and sank down into the sofa cushions.

'About?'

'About staying. I know you wanted to leave, Jake.' She studied him, interested to note that he didn't physically squirm when put under the microscope, but she sensed he was uncomfortable. 'I guess it shows a mark of good breeding. Your parents would be proud.'

'They already are.'

'What does your dad do? Is he a doctor as well?'

'Yes, an obstetrician. My mother is his practice manager.'

'They don't mind working together?'

'No. In fact, they enjoy it.' He paused for a moment. 'Did you enjoy working with Guy?'

'In the beginning. Then life settled down. It's not as though we were in each other's pockets. He saw his patients, I saw mine. Occasionally they overlapped but not very often.' She shrugged. 'I guess we grew further apart than I'd previously thought.'

'You really had no idea he was cheating on you?'

'No, and that's what irritates me the most. When we first met, he loved old cars. He was the one who got me interested. Then, when he realised I shared that interest, he turned his attention to boats. He loved to sail. During the past eight months I've often wondered whether he chose sailing simply because he knew I don't particularly like the sea. I'm not a spend-the-day-at-the-beach type of girl.

Anyway, I continued to learn about cars and every second weekend he went to Adelaide and sailed.' She looked down at her hands and sighed. 'He probably *wasn't* sailing. He was probably living his *other* life as Guy the Playboy.'

Rebekah shook her head. 'I just get so cross with myself now. Why didn't I see what was happening? How could I not have a clue? But every time something…quirky or a little bit different would happen, Guy gave me an explanation even before I asked him. You know, one time he stayed down in Adelaide for three extra days and I didn't question it because he called me up to say a friend of his had gone overboard and he was staying there to look after him. I didn't question it at all.'

'You justified his actions because you loved him,' Jake offered quietly.

'I did. You're so right.'

'Why do you still have your wedding photograph on your dresser?'

She looked at him quizzically.

'Uh…I saw it when I carried you to your room yesterday.'

'Oh.' She met his gaze. 'I keep it there to remind myself never to be a fool again. I was so happy yet all of the time—the last five and a half years of my life—have been an illusion. I thought I knew him. Sure, we had our differences but…' Rebekah looked away and sniffed. 'I need to blow my nose.' She wriggled herself to the edge of the sofa and Jake quickly stood, holding out a hand to help her up. 'Thanks.'

'Becky!' The urgent call came into the house through the back door just as Rebekah quickly let go of Jake's hand.

'What's wrong, Nicole?'

'Margaret's been stung by a wasp and she's not feeling too good.'

'What?' Jake was surprised. 'There are wasps around here?' They all headed for the door, Rebekah grabbing a tissue and blowing her nose as they went. She headed for the kitchen and rummaged around in Gillian's freezer.

'What are you doing?' Jake demanded.

'Getting an ice-pack. Grab my medical bag, will you? It's over near the table.'

He did as she asked and once she'd found the ice-pack, they headed out.

'So why are there wasps?'

'The birds peck at the grapes, wrecking them. The grapes then become overly sweet—'

'Attracting the wasps,' Jake finished.

'There aren't too many about—wasps, I mean. Where's Gillian?' she asked Nicole as the receptionist led the way to where Margaret had been picking grapes.

'She forgot the bratwurst so she's gone to the shops.' Nicole led the way but when Jake saw Margaret, lying on the ground, her body beginning to shake, he ran towards her.

'She's going into shock.' He felt her pulse and checked her breathing. 'Someone get a blanket and call the ambulance. Margaret? Margaret, can you hear me? It's Jake.' The response he received was a whimpered cry. 'She's allergic. Did you know she was allergic?' Jake asked Rebekah.

'No.' Rebekah was working quickly, drawing up a shot of adrenaline before handing it to Jake. As he was crouched down near Margaret, it was easier for him to administer it.

'Oh, Margaret,' Sylvia dithered.

'She'll be fine.' Rebekah slowly knelt on Margaret's other side and applied the ice-pack to the worst affected area. 'The adrenaline Jake's just given her will help settle things down.'

'Will she need to go to hospital?'

'Yes. We'll need to keep her in overnight so we can keep an eye on her.'

'Oh.'

'She'll be fine,' Rebekah reiterated, taking Margaret's pulse.

'How's her pulse rate now?' he asked.

'It feels more normal. There's a portable sphygmomanometer in my bag.'

'Great.' He hauled it out and wrapped the cuff around Margaret's arm before pumping it up to check her BP. 'It's low but the adrenaline should bring it back up soon.'

'How are you feeling now, Margaret?' Rebekah asked as she gently soothed the woman's hair back from her forehead.

'Sleepy.'

'OK, but I need you to stay awake, just for a bit longer. We're going to get you to hospital where you'll be pampered like a princess.'

'Angaston?' The question from Margaret was weak.

'No. Tanunda. That way you'll be nice and close to Sylvia.'

'Sylvia?'

'I'm here. Big sister is here.'

Rebekah watched as Sylvia knelt on the ground and bent to kiss her sister's cheek. She sighed at the beautiful sight. Even at their age, they were still there for each other. She rubbed a hand over her stomach, making a silent promise that she would always be there for her child—regardless. She glanced up and was startled to find Jake watching her. A brief moment, where they seemed to connect on such a personal level. Then he returned his attention back to their patient.

Rebekah followed suit and concentrated on the stings.

The ice-pack had helped reduce the swelling and she now applied a pressure bandage. 'How are you feeling now, Margaret?'

'I've been through worse.'

Sylvia laughed. 'That's the spirit. Childbirth is the most painful thing a woman will ever do. Everything else pales in comparison.'

'Terrific,' Rebekah said blandly, but smiled. '*Now* she tells me.'

Margaret chuckled. 'Too late for you to do anything about it,' she mumbled.

'Ambulance is here,' Nicole called.

Just before they shifted Margaret onto the stretcher, Jake took her blood pressure again and was happy to report it had improved dramatically.

'I'll see you at the hospital.' Rebekah kissed the elderly woman's cheek before the stretcher was manoeuvred into the rear of the ambulance.

Gillian's car pulled into the drive and the other doctor came over. 'What's happening?'

'Margaret got stung by a wasp,' Sylvia announced. 'And had a bad reaction.'

'How are you feeling now?' Gillian asked Margaret.

'Sleepy. Can I sleep?'

'Yes,' Jake replied. 'You're no longer in shock so it's quite fine to have a rest.'

'I'll travel in the ambulance with her,' Sylvia said. 'Could someone bring my car to the hospital?'

'I'll arrange it,' replied Gillian. 'Becky, you and Jake go get Margaret settled in. And, Jake…' Gillian fixed him with a determined look. 'Afterwards, I want you to take Becky home and make sure *she* has a rest.'

'Certainly.'

'Here are your bags, Becky,' Nicole called as she came

running out to the front of the house. She smiled at Jake. 'See *you* tomorrow.'

Jake escorted Rebekah back to his car after thanking Gillian for a wonderful morning.

'Liar,' Rebekah said as they drove behind the ambulance towards the hospital.

'I beg your pardon.'

'You told Gillian you'd had a wonderful morning. I was just calling you a liar.'

He glanced over at her but found her smiling. 'I was being polite.'

'Of course you were. With all of your high-class manners and sensibilities, I should hardly expect anything less from you.'

'Are you teasing me?'

'I most certainly am and I'm enjoying it, too.' She closed her eyes, enjoying the breeze on her face and hair. 'Unlike *some* people in this car, I often tease my friends.'

'I can drop you at home first.'

'Why?'

'To stop you causing trouble. That way, I can tend to Margaret in peace.'

'Very funny.'

'Seriously, though. If you're tired, I can drop you home.'

'It's all right. Margaret might get worried about me if I don't turn up.'

'I'll tell her you're having a rest. It's what pregnant women do.'

'Still, I don't want to worry her. They love to fuss over me.'

'It appears most of the town loves to fuss over you.'

'Yes. It's nice.'

He could imagine it would be for her. She wouldn't take it for granted either. Instead, it was obvious she appreciated every single person's protective attitude towards her and her unborn child.

It didn't take them long to get Margaret settled and once Rebekah was satisfied with her patient's vital signs, Jake took her home.

'Off to bed, sleepyhead.'

'OK.' She stifled a yawn and shuffled off towards her bedroom. 'Wake me if anything exciting happens.'

That was the last Jake saw of her for the rest of the day. He knew she'd wake up an hour or so later and specifically made sure he was out of the house. He went for a drive, enjoying the scenery and the ambience of what was the Barossa Valley. It was relaxing, colourful and a million miles from the hustle and bustle of Sydney. This would be a place where he'd come for a weekend, to enjoy the company of carefully selected friends and carefully selected wines.

Yet here he was, working—with Rebekah. She was far from the sophisticated beauties who were his type yet she had the ability to get inside his head and make him act like a fool.

His mobile phone rang while he was enjoying the architecture of one of the old chateaux Rebekah had mentioned. 'Dr Carson.'

'You're sounding very official, darling. Are you relaxing?'

'Yes, Mum.' He smiled and walked away from the building, heading into the extensive grounds which were beautifully kept. Thankfully, there weren't too many people around at the moment and he soaked up the privacy.

'You're not just saying that to put my mind at ease?'

'No, Mum. How's Dad?'

'Where are you now?'

'I'm actually walking through a lovely garden which surrounds an old chateau. It's beautiful, Mum. You'd love it here.'

'It does sound nice.'

'So how's Dad?'

'Well, that's part of the reason I called.'

Jake stood still. 'What's happened?' He gripped the phone tighter and clenched his jaw.

'Nothing. Nothing bad. Your father was in a car acci-dent—but he's OK,' she rushed on. 'He has a seat-belt bruise and a bit of whiplash and a broken ankle but that's all.'

'What! He broke his ankle?' Jake could feel his blood pressure start to rise.

'Calm down, Jake. Breathe normally.'

'Mum! Tell me exactly what happened.'

'The car was hit from behind rather forcefully which propelled our car forward into the one in front.'

'Were you with him?'

'No, dear. He was coming back from the hospital this morning after doing a ward round.'

'I'm coming home.'

'No. Really, Jake. He's fine.'

'Where are you?'

'At the hospital. He's having a cast put on right now. They wanted to keep him in overnight for observation but of course he's kicked up a big stink.'

'So the fracture doesn't require surgery?'

'It's a clean break.'

'Good. He should stay in hospital.'

'Oh, he'll be staying all right. I won't allow him to dis-charge himself.'

'Try and make him behave, Mum—at least for the next twenty-four hours.'

'I promise.'

'Keep me informed.'

'I will, dear.'

'I'll come home if I have to.'

'I don't think that's necessary but I'll certainly tell your father that if he doesn't do as he's told, he'll more than likely cause you concern and we all know you need to keep calm.'

'Hmm.' Jake frowned, forcing himself to unclench every muscle he was tensing. 'I love you, Mum.'

'I love you, too, son. Bye.'

Jake ended the call and shook his head. He'd been gone from Sydney for two days. *Two days*—and something had gone wrong. He shouldn't have left. He should be there, for his parents. Again, he forced himself to relax. His cardiologist had prescribed lots of rest and relaxation, as well as an immediate change in workload. 'Type A,' he muttered as he stalked back to the car, but even as he said the words, he remembered that aching pain around his chest. The way it had travelled along his arm and how he'd been utterly helpless to do anything about it. He slowed his pace.

He drove back to Rebekah's house via the scenic route, forcing himself to absorb its beauty and natural charm. When he returned it was night-time and again there was no sign of her. He went to his room, showered and got ready for bed. He had clinic tomorrow morning and house calls in the afternoon. Although the pace was different from Sydney, the patients still had complaints which were real and he owed it to them to be alert. He called the hospital and received an update from the doctor treating his father. Satisfied his father had remained in hospital, Jake rang off.

He glanced over at the clock. It was only nine-thirty and here he was, tucked up in bed. If his parents could see him now, they'd laugh. Perhaps it was the manual labour he'd done that morning which was making him feel so exhausted. 'Or maybe it's the way you can't seem to get Rebekah out of your head,' he muttered, and buried his head beneath the pillow, forcing his thoughts in a completely different direction.

Four-fifteen. The digital clock had to be wrong. He'd been tossing and turning for hours. *Surely* it was almost morning! He flung the covers back, climbed from the bed and pulled on his robe. He needed a drink and not just water from the bathroom tap.

Jake headed out to the kitchen, stopping in the doorway to check the coast was clear. Had Rebekah been up already? He glanced around the darkened room. There were no signs that anyone had been in the kitchen. No jars of chocolate spread left out, no knives on the draining-board. Maybe she'd just come out for a drink.

Regardless, the kitchen was empty now. Jake hurried over to the sink and filled the kettle with water before switching it on. While he was waiting he looked through the herbal teas she had in the cupboard and decided on Cubby Wubby Womb Room tea as it prescribed a relaxing outcome.

He'd always thought he was adept at handling his stress levels. He didn't smoke. He worked out regularly. Watched his intake of fats and sugars and enjoyed a glass of wine every now and then. His work offered the challenge he relished and his research had completed the balance. Yet since he'd arrived in the Barossa—correction, since he'd met Rebekah Sanderson—his stress levels appeared to have risen somewhat. It was extremely rare that he had trouble sleeping and not once, since he'd set foot in this house, had he slept through the night.

'Morning.' Rebekah shuffled sleepily into the room,

scratching her stomach. 'Junior's doing the morning exercise routine a little later today. Maybe there's hope.'

'For what?' Did she have to look so incredibly gorgeous with her hair all messed up and stuck out at funny angles? Her robe was hanging open, her feet were in those ridiculous fluffy slippers. She looked…good enough to eat. Jake cleared his throat, willing the kettle to hurry up and boil.

'That Junior's going to grow out of being an early riser.'

Jake smiled at her words. 'Wishful thinking?'

She returned his smile. 'Something like that. What are you drinking?' She peered into his mug on her way past him to the fridge.

'Herbal tea.'

'Mmm. Sounds good.'

Without saying another word, Jake took another cup down and added another tea-bag. 'Sugar or honey?'

'Honey, please.' She collected a ring of Camembert out of the fridge and headed over to the bread bin where she retrieved a small baguette. 'Hungry?'

'No.'

She closed the bread bin, picked up a knife and a plate before seating herself at the table. 'So why can't you sleep?' She spread some cheese onto the bread.

Jake looked at her, his mind filtering through several different things he could say. Thankfully, the kettle switched itself off and he almost pounced on it, pouring water into the waiting cups.

He made the tea and when he placed her cup down in front of her, Rebekah noticed his face was strained. 'What's wrong, Jake?'

He didn't sit down at the table but instead leaned against the bench, his cup between his hands. 'My father. He was in a car accident.'

'Oh. Is he all right?'

'Yes. Fractured ankle, whiplash and seat-belt bruise.'

'Glad to hear he was wearing one. And your mother?'

'She wasn't with him. She called me while I was out. I'm worried about them.'

'If you need to go back to Sydney—'

'It's all right. Mum will keep me informed.'

'OK.' She took a sip of her tea. 'Mmm, this is nice.'

He turned towards his end of the house. 'See you later in the morning.'

'You're not going to stay and keep me company?'

She'd asked him that before and he'd stayed, and because he'd stayed, he'd become better acquainted with her. If he stayed again, his knowledge would increase and for the moment he knew all he wanted to know about his colleague…far too much, in fact…far more than he knew about people he'd worked with for over a decade. She was an open, honest, giving person and he knew if he didn't stay, at least for a few minutes while he drank his tea, and keep her company, she might be offended.

'Sure.' He turned back to the table and sat a few seats away from her.

Rebekah finished eating and took another sip of her tea. 'I called through to the hospital to check on Margaret. She's sleeping soundly. All her vital signs are fine.'

'Good.'

'Was yesterday really as bad as you thought it might be?'

'It wasn't *bad*.'

'You're just not used to it.'

'No.'

'Well, I'm glad you stayed, especially for Margaret's sake.'

'You would have been able to handle that with your hands tied behind your back,' he commented.

'Thank you. That's nice of you to say so but I have to

tell you, in my present condition, I definitely can't move as fast as you. It's frustrating.'

'I'm sure it is. Soon, though, it will all be over—'

'And I'll be frustrated for a different reason,' she finished with a wry grimace.

'I thought you were looking forward to it.'

'I am. I'm getting desperate to meet my child. To hold it in my arms. To smother it with kisses. But the fact remains that being a single mother is not going to be an easy trick. Then there's the clinic and what if I need time off after you leave and we can't get another locum? What if something goes wrong with the birth? I'm happy with my level of medical care, don't get me wrong, but I just have all these thoughts constantly running through my head and I can't seem to stop them.

'What if my waters break when I'm at the shops or at a patient's house? What if I go over my due date and I have to be induced? What if I have a reaction to the medication? What if I need a C-section and I'm the only one here who's licensed to do one? What if it's so painful I can't cope? What if Gillian can't make it and I don't have a birthing partner? What if something's wrong with the baby? Should I have had that glass of wine? Am I going to be a good mother?' Her voice had risen to a crescendo and she buried her head in her hands, her shoulders shaking as she started to cry.

Jake was horrified. Not at what she'd said but how concerned she was about everything. He'd had no idea her stress level was this high and it could seriously affect her blood pressure.

'And those questions are only the tip of the iceberg,' she sniffed, raising her head again. 'What if I can't cope with the baby and can't return to work? What if I have postnatal depression? What if I can't do this and end up rejecting the child, like my parents rejected me?'

'Your parents rejected you?'

'Not in so many words.' She sniffed. 'I have a younger brother and it was clear once he was born that they favoured him over me.' She shrugged. 'It was just the way it was. I always seemed to be an afterthought.'

'That won't happen with you and your baby. You're not that type of person.' His tone was forceful.

Tears continued to trickle down her cheeks and she patted the pockets of her dressing-gown for a handkerchief. Jake quickly took a box of tissues from the window-ledge and brought them over to her.

'Thanks.'

He sat down beside her and took her hand in his. 'It's natural to have doubts, Rebekah. Very natural.'

'I know, but what if some of them come true?'

'The part about you rejecting your child will *never* come true.'

'And you know this how? You hardly know me, Jake.'

'I know you well enough to answer that question with absolute clarity. Your child is already loved, already wanted, already needed.' He squeezed her hand, desperately wanting to reassure her that she was going to be all right.

Rebekah withdrew her hand and blew her nose. Jake reached out and brushed a few strands of hair from her face, tucking them behind her ear.

'You'll be fine. You're a survivor, Rebekah. You and the baby are going to be great.'

'Really?' She so desperately wanted to believe it.

Jake leaned closer and cupped her cheek in his hand. 'Yes.' His answer was one hundred per cent positive. 'Regardless of what life throws at you, you make the best of it. I may not know you as well as the other people in this town do but I know you're a giving and generous person. A rare, precious gem, shining brightly in the face of adversity.'

Her lower lip started to tremble and a fresh bout of tears started to flow at his words. He took a tissue and tenderly wiped them away, the action endearing him to her even more. 'Thank you,' she whispered and, leaning that little bit closer, pressed her lips to his.

The instant they touched, they stared at each other, eyes as wide as saucers—both registering the earth-shattering sensations which coursed through their bodies.

Her intention had been merely to thank him for his words, words that had helped heal a few cracks in her heart, yet the instant her mouth had touched his, her mind had registered what she was doing.

The heat, the power, the strength she felt in that one nanosecond was enough to spur her on, enough to urge her to take a chance. Her mind had registered his scent when she'd first walked into the kitchen but now, being so close, everything was heightened.

She breathed in, a deep, shaky breath, before sighing into the kiss. She'd shocked him, she knew, but still it was something she'd thought about doing almost since the first moment she'd set eyes on him, but was he going to fight it?

With a muffled groan, he cupped her face in his hands and kissed her ardently, the pent-up passion and desire surging out of him.

He couldn't stop himself.

He needed this.

CHAPTER FOUR

SHE was sweeter than anything he'd ever tasted in his life!

A mixture of the cheese, the bread, the tea, the honey—and her own pure, honest, sweetness. Rebekah filled his senses completely and Jake could feel himself going under, wanting more, needing more—and she didn't disappoint.

He had thought that one simple kiss might get her out of his system, that one simple kiss might help him to sleep at night, that one simple kiss would be all he would ever need from her.

He was wrong!

Groaning, he leaned closer, sifting his fingers through her hair until they fisted at the rear of her head, immobilising her. She didn't mind at all and gave herself up to the emotions raging inside. She hadn't meant for things to go this far, for them to get so out of control, but now that they had, she savoured every moment.

This was passion as she'd never felt it before. How could he stir such incredible longing with one hungry, hot kiss? It was unbelievable and she felt as though she were floating…lifted up on the wings of desire. Desire which she was thrilled to discover was mutual.

As though he wanted to slow things down a little, he shifted gears, his mouth moving over hers in a sensual caress—a lover's caress. She wasn't sure how she was supposed to cope. She had thought she was on fire before with his hot and hungry kisses but now…now the flame had been fanned into a slow all-consuming fire—one that was taking her senses up on an internal climb so high, she felt as though she'd erupt like bright fireworks. Fire-stars, she'd called them as a child, and now the term seemed appropriate for how he was making her feel. Fire-stars bursting brightly, one after the other as his mouth moved carefully and meticulously over hers.

It was as though he had to memorise ever inch of her. You do, he told himself, because this moment in time needs to last you for ever. Now that he'd done it, now that he'd given in to the urge to kiss her, he wanted it to be thorough. Thorough enough to last him a lifetime because he was positive no other woman had affected him so mind-blowingly as Rebekah.

He groaned, knowing he needed to slow things down. Not only had he wanted to savour her but he knew if they kept this frantic pace—both of them racing along like an out-of-control freight train—it would soon be impossible to stop.

So he slowed it down.

The way she responded, not holding back, had him losing his mind completely. He broke his mouth free and pressed kisses to her face, his fingers loosening in her hair but still holding her head where he needed it—next to his. He shifted his chair closer before nuzzling her earlobe. Her hair was soft and silky to his touch as he brushed it out of the way so he could rain kisses on the sensitive hollow of her luscious neck.

'Mmm,' she moaned, and shivered slightly as goose-bumps broke out over her skin. It was torture. Sheer, sweet, torture and she never wanted it to stop. With an impatience she couldn't control, she willed his lips to stop the pleasurable torment and return to her mouth. 'Kiss me,' she whispered, the words hardly audible—but he heard them.

He decided to tease her for a bit longer and nibbled the other side of her neck, enjoying the way she moaned and shivered beneath his touch. Finally, when he, too, was impatient for her touch, he brought his mouth back to hers.

They met as old friends, eager to get reacquainted, eager to continue with their journey. Even though it was all still new, he felt as though he'd been kissing her for ever. The taste of her was genuine and her scent was a natural and powerful aphrodisiac.

Never had he expected such a gamut of emotions when he'd given in to the urge to kiss her. Her tongue lightly outlined his lips and he heard himself groan again, amazed at how this woman could override all his warning signals and shoot him straight through the heart.

The heart!

The thought was enough to make him pull back. Jake cupped her face in his hands and stared down into her eyes, both of them breathing heavily.

Rebekah's blue eyes were glazed with pent-up frustration and desire, small swirls of dark indigo surrounding her dilated pupils. Her lips were slightly swollen and pink—irresistible. Just gazing at her now had him wanting her all over again.

Jake wanted to give in but knew if he did, there was no way he'd have the will-power to stop things from taking their inevitable course. They kept gazing at each other as their heart rates gradually returned to normal, her eyelids gradually lowering as she sighed contentedly.

'Sleepy,' she murmured, and couldn't help the yawn which escaped. She smiled. 'I'm going back to bed now.' Tenderly, she brushed one hand across his cheek before pushing her chair back and standing. Smothering another yawn, Jake watched as she shuffled out of the room and disappeared to her end of the house.

He sat there, like a stunned mullet, listening to the sounds as she went to the bathroom before getting into her bed. How could his hearing be so acute, so in tune to every move she made? He'd kissed her. Rebekah—he'd kissed her! She was his colleague. She was pregnant. What had he been thinking?

He hadn't.

Plain and simple—he hadn't.

Shaking his head in disgust at himself, he stood, putting the chairs into their proper places before clearing up the mess and heading to his own end of the house. This wasn't going to work. He needed to find somewhere else to stay because he'd been in the same house as Rebekah for only three nights and already it was becoming a problem.

Although, if he did rent a small place of his own, it would get the entire town gossiping. At the moment, they all seemed quite happy he was there to look after Rebekah. Hadn't anyone guessed that he and Rebekah were undeniably attracted to one another? Were they all blind? The chemistry between them was evident. Or maybe people were already talking about them but he just hadn't heard it. That was probably more to the point.

By him being here—in her house—it not only provided twenty-four-hour care for their pregnant doctor but it might also be useful in case he and Rebekah wanted to fall in love. That way, she wouldn't be on her own any more and he could quit his job, his life in Sydney and move to the Barossa to live happily ever after. That's probably what they were all expecting. Well, they would be disappointed.

Jake lay on his bed, hands behind his head as he stared up at the ceiling, forcing himself to think about something else, *anything* else…like his research project. Once he'd collated the data Guy had gathered, he'd be one step closer to writing a proposal for the second stage of the research— one that would be implemented in country and rural areas around Australia. It was a big ask—but he *had* to pull it off.

Six months. He was here for six months. Enough time to get his thoughts together, gradually lower his stress levels so he could return to Sydney, relaxed, refreshed and ready to apply for the position of director of paediatrics at the hospital. He'd been working towards it for—well, for ever and he was determined it would come to fruition.

He'd planned to secure the directorship, look around for a suitable wife and settle down to his life. All he had to do was find the right woman and therein lay the problem with Rebekah. She was *not* the right woman. She had been married to Guy von Appen—a man he'd thought he'd known. She was expecting Guy's baby and she lived and worked in a sleepy little town. *Completely* different to what he wanted in a wife.

Jake closed his eyes and shook his head in exasperation. She'd done it again. Taken over his thoughts without permission.

'Definitely not the right woman,' he reiterated, before forcing his thoughts elsewhere.

Rebekah woke feeling…incredible!

As she climbed from her bed and headed to the bathroom, she started to sing 'Oh, What a Beautiful Morning' because it was true. The autumn sun was out, the leaves were rustling in the trees and the sky was a lovely pale blue colour with a few white, fluffy clouds. Perfect!

She sighed deeply, amazed at how good she felt…and it was all thanks to Jake Carson. After the kiss they'd shared, she'd slept soundly for three hours straight! She'd woken up in the exact same position she'd gone to sleep in.

'Thank you, blossom,' she told her baby, 'for letting Mummy have a good sleep. Do you feel good too, my honey?' She stroked her stomach as she showered and dressed. 'We're going to relax this morning because Jake's doing the clinic. Then we'll go and visit some people this afternoon so we can introduce him to today's house-call list.'

When she went out into the kitchen to have breakfast, she found it tidy. She smiled. He was such a sweetie for putting everything away. She started the coffee, wondering if he'd managed to get to sleep or whether he was still out to it. Either way, she needed to eat.

After having a bowl of cereal, there was still no sign of Jake. Clinic started in half an hour and she didn't want him to oversleep on his first day. Cautiously, she entered his part of the house, called his name softly. There was no sound coming from the bathroom and at his bedroom door she knocked before slowly opening the door.

There was no sign of him.

His bed was made and the room was neat and tidy. Had he gone to the clinic already? Had he gone out for a run? Feeling as though she were trespassing, she headed back to the kitchen and reminded herself that he was a big boy and could take care of himself.

'Good morning,' Nicole said when Rebekah hurried through the clinic door. 'I thought you were going to have a rest this morning. You know, take it easy because Jake's here.'

'He is? Here, I mean.'

'Yes. He was here when I arrived. I think he's checking over the case notes of the people he's seeing today. What a man.' Nicole sighed dramatically and clutched her hand to her chest.

Rebekah went down the corridor towards her consulting room.

'What are you doing here?' Gillian asked, stopping her. 'You're supposed to be off your feet and resting.'

'I...uh...' What was she supposed to say? That she hadn't been able to find Jake that morning? That she was concerned about him? That her day wouldn't feel right until she'd laid eyes on him? '—forgot something in my consulting room and wanted to get it before Jake started the clinic.'

'Oh.' Gillian eased back and looked at her. 'You look...lovely this morning, Becky. Pregnancy really does suit you.'

She smiled easily at her friend. 'Thanks.' She pushed open the door to her consulting room. She looked in, realised Jake was on the phone and quickly apologised. 'Sorry,' she whispered as she came into the room and shut the door.

'Excuse me a moment.' He placed the receiver on the desk and looked at her. 'Problem?'

'Uh...no. Sorry, I didn't mean to barge in.' She smiled at him, feeling instantly better just from seeing him. He was dressed in a charcoal pinstripe suit with a pale blue shirt and university tie. There was not a hair out of place on his head and his eyes were sharp and cool. Professional. The urge to ruffle him up a bit was almost overpowering. Her smile increased at the thought.

'Rebekah?' She was gazing at him in such a playful way he wanted to cross to her side and kiss her senseless. That was *not* going to happen. He sat up straighter in his chair, glad the barrier of the desk was between them.

'Sorry. Just needed to...uh...pick up this textbook.' She walked over to her bookshelf and grabbed a book before heading back to the door. 'I'll let you get back to your phone call. See you this afternoon.'

Her parting smile was encompassing, wrapping around him like a comfortable blanket on a windy day. He clenched his jaw tightly and waited a full three beats after she'd closed the door behind her before picking up the phone again.

'Mum?'

'Who was that?'

'Rebekah Sanderson. The woman I'm locuming for.'

'Oh. If she's there, why are you locuming for her? I thought you went because that young man doing the research for you died.'

'That's right, only it turns out the job was to cover Rebekah while she's on maternity leave.'

'Oh. Has she had the baby yet?'

'No. She's due in the next few weeks.'

'How exciting. Is she pretty?'

'What does it matter?'

'She sure sounds pretty. What does her husband do?' Jake explained how Guy fitted into the picture and his mother was naturally concerned. 'That poor, poor woman. You must stay there and help her, Jake.'

'I will, Mum.'

'Oh, by the way, a Professor Libskee stopped by your father's room this morning and said he wanted to set up a meeting with you in a few weeks' time. I told him I'd pass on the message.'

'Excellent.'

'This is about your research project, isn't it,' she stated. 'Well, I don't want you working day and night to put something together, Jake. I want you alive, not plugged into some heart monitor.'

'I won't overdo it, Mum. I promise. You take care of Dad and keep in touch. Here, let me give you the number here at the clinic and at the house.' He recited Rebekah's home number. 'Call me if you need anything.'

'I will. You keep relaxing.'

'Yes, Mum.' He chuckled and rang off. He'd been doing a fine job of relaxing while on the phone to his mother—until Rebekah had walked in. His gaze had flown instantly to her peach-pink lips and the memory of the incredible kisses they'd shared only a few hours ago had been so real he had been able to taste her all over again.

He closed his eyes and rubbed his fingers in little circular motions against his temples. The intercom on the desk buzzed and Nicole announced his first patient.

Glad of the distraction, he pigeonholed all thoughts of Rebekah and went out to call his first patient through.

'You're looking much better, Margaret.' Rebekah shook the thermometer down. 'Temperature is normal, blood pressure is normal, heart rate is normal.'

'Can I go home?'

'I don't see why not. What do you think, Sylvia? Able to cope with Margaret milking the experience for all it's worth?'

Sylvia laughed. 'Oh, yes, Dr Sanderson. I'm well used to my little sister's ways.'

'Who are you calling little?' Margaret bantered. 'I'm two centimetres taller than you.'

'But you're three years younger, dear.' Sylvia smiled at her sister. 'Come on, let's get you out of bed and packed to go home.'

Margaret stayed where she was, staring at Rebekah. 'You know, dear, you look…different today.'

'Yes, I thought the same when she walked in the door,' replied Sylvia.

Rebekah knew she'd been walking around with a goofy grin on her face all morning—well, at least after she'd discovered Jake's whereabouts. 'It's the pregnancy,' she offered. 'Women usually glow in the last trimester.'

'I'm certain *I* never glowed like you are today,' Margaret scoffed.

'It's that young doctor from Sydney.' Sylvia nodded wisely.

'Yes. We saw the way you were looking at each other yesterday.'

'What way?' Rebekah couldn't help but laugh.

'The way a woman looks at a man when she's interested. We may be old but we're not senile,' Sylvia announced sternly.

'No. Nor blind,' Margaret added. 'It's lovely, dear, that you've found another man.'

'A good one this time. One who won't cheat on you.'

'How can you be so sure of that?'

'You've got to trust again, dear,' Sylvia said softly. 'But never mind. It will happen when you're ready.'

'Is he a good kisser?'

'Margaret!' Rebekah wasn't sure whether to laugh or cry. She could also feel herself beginning to blush.

'What? You're not going to give a dying woman her last wish?'

Rebekah laughed. 'You are *not* dying and if that was your last wish, it would be a pretty sad one.' She shook her head in amazement at the two women. 'I'm going to continue with my round so why don't you get packed? Call the clinic if you have any worries, but from what I've seen of your vital signs, you've made a good recovery.'

Rebekah headed out of the room but even in the corridor she heard Margaret crow, 'Notice how she didn't answer the question.'

'We'd better keep quiet,' Sylvia agreed. 'We don't want to scare him off. She deserves a good man.'

Rebekah sighed and then laughed before going to see her

other three patients. Once she was done, Monica sent her
home to rest, threatening to tell Gillian if she didn't.

'I'm going,' Rebekah promised, and headed across the
road. Her step was light, her hair felt free, the silly school-
girl smile was plastered to her face. She wasn't going to
deny her attraction to him, or the way his kisses had curled
her toes and made her heart pound out of control. Jake
Carson had done a marvellous thing by kissing her—he'd
restored her self-esteem.

Guy had done a good job of killing it and she hadn't
thought she'd ever get it back again. When she'd learned
he'd been sleeping with other women, she'd been devastated. Had she been so inadequate? Hadn't she pleased him
in the bedroom? She'd questioned herself over and over
until her head had spun with unanswered questions.

Now, though, Jake had kissed her and, wow…what a
kiss!

He was an incredibly handsome man and he'd *chosen* to
kiss her. He'd *wanted* to kiss her and had obviously *enjoyed*
kissing her. Even though she was enormously pregnant, felt
uncomfortable most of the time and wished her hair wasn't
so lifeless, none of that had mattered one bit to him. That,
in itself, had helped improve her self-esteem.

Jake Carson liked her—for her.

CHAPTER FIVE

VIVID dreams of being held and kissed by Jake had Rebekah waking from her rest refreshed and ready for afternoon house calls. While she had a quick bite to satisfy the baby, she smiled as she recalled how he'd taken her in his arms—of course, she'd not been pregnant in her dream—and crushed her body against the length of his with palpable impatience.

'Yummy.' She licked her lips and then laughed, trying to figure out whether the word applied to the food or her thoughts. 'Both,' she decided after a moment, and laughed again. With a spring in her step, which she enjoyed while it lasted, she headed over to the clinic to pull out the necessary patient files. 'Anyone else been added to the list, Nicole?'

'No. You have three patients.'

'Great. Is Jake almost done?'

'Just finishing up with his last patient. Gosh, that man's a dish. I tell you, every time he came out to the waiting room to escort a patient through, all the women sighed in appreciation.'

Rebekah could well believe it.

'Can we get him to stay longer?' Nicole pleaded urgently.

'No. He's already told me he just wants to do his job and then leave, which is all he's been asked to do.'

'Pity.' Nicole sighed dramatically. 'I envy you, Rebekah. You get to see him in the morning and in the evening and you've probably had breakfast and dinner together.' She sat up straighter. 'Does he snore?'

'How should I know? He sleeps down the other end of the house.' Rebekah didn't want to talk about him, not like this and not with Nicole. She picked up her medical bag and took it through to the room where the drug cupboard was located. Glad of the silence, she checked the medication off against the patients they'd be seeing this afternoon.

'Sorry I'm late, Rebekah.'

She spun around to face Jake, a little startled by his sudden appearance. 'That's OK. I know what it's like.'

'You all packed and ready to go?'

She relocked the drug cupboard. 'Sure am.'

'Great. Let's get going.' He turned and walked away.

He was brisk and eager and she wondered if he wanted his time with her to be over and done with as soon as possible. Those were insecure thoughts—the voice in her head was stern. You are no longer an insecure person. You are an emancipated woman who is taking control of her time and her life. If you want to kiss Jake Carson, then you're entitled to do it—if he doesn't have any objections, that is. She followed him out of the clinic, waving goodbye to an envious Nicole before heading back to her house where his car was parked.

He certainly hadn't had any objections earlier this morning. She rubbed her stomach thoughtfully and smiled like the cat who'd eaten the cream. In fact, he'd been very enthusiastic and the knowledge made the warm fuzzy feeling return once more.

'Let me take that for you.' Without waiting for her to answer, Jake took her medical bag and put it in the car before holding the passenger door open for her. He waited for her to seat herself and put her seat belt on before heading around to the driver's side.

'So how was clinic?' she asked as he slid behind the wheel and started the engine.

'Routine.'

'Good. Go right.'

He pulled out of the driveway. 'Who's first on the list?'

'Hetty James. She's almost fifty-two and has been suffering from stress. She's had a spate of mouth ulcers but— Oh, you met her husband the other day. Clive—the cleaner. The one swinging the floor polisher.'

'Manuka honey?'

'Correct. Hetty needs to slow down and smell the roses but instead she works herself into a frenzy. She almost didn't speak to me again when I prescribed four weeks off work.' Rebekah shook her head. 'What that woman needs to help her unwind are grandchildren but there's no chance of that on the horizon.'

'Let me guess. You're going to let her help you with your baby.'

'And why not? I need help, Hetty needs to slow down. It's a win-win situation.'

'And what about your child?'

'It wins as well because it will be smothered with love.' Rebekah shook her hair free in the wind and closed her eyes. 'I doubt anyone could ever suffer from being over-loved.'

The words had been said softly and he silently berated her parents for treating her the way they had. He glanced across and was mesmerised by the way her hair was flowing gently on the breeze, her long neck exposed in the autumn sunshine. Perfect for kissing.

It wasn't the first time she'd thrown her head back like that and he was beginning to expect it from her. Had she any idea how incredibly beautiful she was? He glanced over at her a few times, wishing she would stop distracting him from driving.

'Go right at the next street,' she said without opening her eyes.

'Sure?'

'Positive.'

'So why can't Hetty come to the clinic to see you?'

'No. No way. That would mean we miss out on some amazing home cooking.'

He frowned but didn't say anything else. Once he'd made the turn, she said, 'Third house on the left. The one with all the garden gnomes.'

'Any gnome-napping ever happened?'

She lifted her head and opened her eyes. They were sparkling with merriment and the corners of her mouth pulled upwards into a smile. 'In Tanunda?' She raised her eyebrows and then laughed. 'I think Clive would love it.' She waited until the car had stopped before opening her door.

Jake rushed around and helped her out. 'Thanks. I'm looking forward to the day when I can get in and out of a car without such a hassle.' He let go of her hand the instant she was standing and steady on her feet. Her smile faded and she glanced at him from beneath her lashes as he retrieved her bag. Was it her imagination or was he in a strange mood?

'Shall we go in?' She knocked on the door and it was flung open almost immediately by a woman dressed in a casual suit, her dark hair immaculate and her make-up perfect.

'Come in, Rebekah. Oh, and you, too, Dr Carson.'

'Thank you, Hetty.'

'Tea? Coffee? I've made some fresh scones.'

'That would be lovely,' Rebekah responded with a wide grin at Jake. 'You *must* try one of Hetty's scones, especially when they're fresh from the oven. They are mouth-watering.'

Hetty literally beamed. Rebekah hadn't seen her smile like that in a very long time. They sat in the 'good' lounge room on plastic-covered sofa chairs. Just relax, Hetty, just relax, she prayed. Hetty's recent tests had shown her mouth wasn't the only place where an ulcer might be brewing.

'Have all my test results come back in?' Hetty asked, getting straight to the point.

'Not yet but I'm fairly certain you do have an ulcer in your stomach.'

'Won't the manuka honey help that, too? After all, it's worked extremely well for my mouth ulcers.'

'Yes, so Clive was telling me. That's great news.'

'When can I go back to work?'

'Not until we've started treatment for your stomach ulcer and I can't do that until the tests are confirmed.'

Hetty crossed her arms and sighed huffily. There goes her blood pressure, Rebekah thought.

'Rebekah, you were right. These scones are incredible. Hetty, you're a marvel in the kitchen.' Jake smiled at their patient and Rebekah watched as the other woman instantly relaxed, a slight blush colouring her cheeks. Did he have this effect on *all* women?

'If it's not too much trouble, may I have the recipe to pass on to my mother? She loves to do a bit of baking in the kitchen. Says it relaxes her.'

'Of course,' Hetty replied.

'So what relaxes you, Jake?' Rebekah asked. It was a hunch and one she was going to follow.

'Er…' He glared at her for a moment and cleared his throat. 'I like long drives.'

'Do you get much chance to do them in Sydney?'

'No.' His tone was clipped and she knew she'd just

rubbed him up the wrong way—but she'd done it for a reason.

'Jake's a type A—like you, Hetty. All the classic symptoms. You know, pacing when you have time on your hands, wanting to just knuckle down and get the job done, and although he *knows* how he should relax, he often doesn't do it.'

Jake clenched his jaw, his eyes narrow with anger. He couldn't believe she was saying this in front of a patient, although he wasn't sure which bothered him more—the fact that she was openly talking about it, or the fact that she'd read him so easily.

'Oh, I'm so pleased there's someone else around like me,' Hetty remarked. 'But I do want to point out, young Becky, that there's nothing wrong with knuckling down and getting the job done. If more people did it and did it well, then perhaps life would be easier all round.'

'Good point.' Rebekah nodded as she reached for another scone.

'The thing I'm finding the hardest, Dr Carson, is being told to stop. I love my job—I'm the personal assistant to the solicitor in town and have been for the last twenty-five years. Just because I'm getting older, it doesn't mean I'm less capable. I'm responsible for all the office staff and run the entire business like a well-oiled machine. Now Becky tells me I must slow down or my body will slow down for me.'

'She's right,' Jake replied. 'Unfortunately, she's right.'

'Is that one of the reasons why you've come to Tanunda for six months?' Hetty sipped her cup of tea.

'Yes. I…er…had a mild twinge a month ago and since then I've been on the ''slow down'' plan.'

'Twinge? What does that mean?'

Jake looked at Rebekah but as she shoved another piece

of scone into her mouth he knew it was up to him to answer. She did, however, smile sweetly at him and it made him want to wring her pretty little neck.

'I had a very mild warning—a small heart attack was the term my cardiologist used.'

Rebekah swallowed over her mouthful which had instantly turned to stone at his words. She'd had no idea his type A status was that serious. Hetty gasped and covered her mouth with her hand.

'Oh, Dr Carson. You *must* take it easy, then. As hard as it is for people like us to slow down, we *must* do it. Oh, dear.'

'I didn't mean to upset you,' he said quickly. He didn't want to look at Rebekah, knowing he'd probably see something like pity in her gaze. His colleagues and friends had looked at him like that and it had made him angry. They'd started to treat him as though he'd had an incurable disease. His secretary had even started cutting back on his private consulting appointments specifically to help him out. He shook his head and forced himself to have another swallow from his tea-cup.

'I'm not upset, dear, merely concerned. Not only for you but for myself as well. I've had stomach problems and Rebekah says that's where I put all my stress. My heart, thankfully, is good.'

Rebekah sat there, watching the two of them and hoping this would now get the message through to Hetty.

'Right, then, Hetty,' Rebekah said, deciding Jake had done his job and now needed a break. 'Let's take your blood pressure and have a look at your mouth and throat. I'll then ring the path lab in Adelaide to see how much longer those results will be.'

'I guess that's all I can ask for now,' Hetty sighed.

'Yes. Sorry.' She got on with the examination and was

pleasantly surprised at the lower BP rate. 'Very good. It's coming down. Whatever you're doing is working.'

'I'm baking. Poor Clive has biscuits and scones coming out of his ears.'

'Well, if you've got too many, send some to the poor starving doctors. The baby loves yummy snacks,' Rebekah prompted, and Hetty laughed.

'I'll make sure I do that. Give me something to occupy my time during my enforced stay here.' Even though the last three words had been said with emphasis, Hetty smiled.

It wasn't much longer before they took their leave and once they were back in the car and Rebekah had given Jake directions, she thanked him for his help.

'You were like a destressing machine for her. I think it's mainly thanks to you that we'll be getting delicious food from Hetty.'

He merely nodded politely.

'What is it?'

'Pardon?'

'Why are you cross with me?'

'Who said I was cross with you?'

'I can read your body language, Jake.'

'Know me well, do you?'

'That's not what I meant.'

He stopped the car at a red light and turned to face her. 'You used me, Rebekah. You used my personal situation to help out a patient.'

She felt as though he'd slapped her. 'I understand and apologise. The main reason I brought it up with Hetty was to get the point across that slowing down was necessary. She now also feels that she's not the only one in this town who is having to do this. You're here, you're doing it as well—which, I might add, I commend you for.'

'I don't want it discussed around the town.'

'I promise I won't say a word to anyone else—and, I might add, neither will Hetty. She's not the type to gossip.'

Jake glanced at her, unsure.

'My lips are sealed.' She drew her fingers across her lips in a zipper action. Jake completely surprised her by laughing. 'What?'

'I didn't think it would last long.'

'Meaning?'

'You're a chatter-box, Rebekah. A social person who likes to talk. Nothing wrong with it but don't make promises you can't keep.'

She smiled, glad he was out of his brooding mood. 'I didn't mean I was going to stop talking altogether, just that I wouldn't mention—'

'I know. I know.' How had she managed to get him out of his mood so easily? He was surprised how light and relaxed he felt, his annoyance fading away on the autumn breeze. 'Which way now?'

She gave him the directions to Leo's house.

'You only saw him on Friday. Why are you checking up on him two and a half days later?'

'Because he's my friend.'

'I'm beginning to think these house calls are more for your benefit than the patients'.'

Rebekah laughed. 'Caught me out.'

As Jake drove, he shook his head in bewilderment. He'd decided that morning that he was going to remain aloof, to well and truly keep his distance from Rebekah. Yet here he was, only a few hours later, teasing and laughing with her.

He didn't want to laugh with her. If he did that, he would come to know her, to like her, more than he already did, but the other thing, which perhaps annoyed him more, was that he wasn't sticking to his plan. He was a man who always stuck to his plan. His plans, which were *always* rationally evaluated and logically processed *always* worked but only when he stuck to them. Why was it so hard around this woman?

Leo greeted not only Rebekah but Jake as well like an old friend.

'Come in, come in. Yer running nicely to time.'

'Yes. Miracles of miracles. I'll be back in a moment,' she said, excusing herself and walking down the hallway of Leo's home.

'I reckon the doc knows where the toilet is in everyone's house.' Leo chuckled as he put the kettle on. 'Tea, Dr Carson?'

Jake was full of Hetty's delicious scones but, remembering what Rebekah had said about Leo being lonely, he found himself nodding. 'Tea would be great.'

'Good.' They chatted for a few minutes about the weather before Rebekah returned.

'Have you been taking your medicine, Leo?'

'Straight to the point. That's our Becky.'

'Well, have you?'

'Milk and sugar, dear?'

'You know how I take my tea so quit stalling.'

'Yes, I've been taking them like I promised.'

'And?'

'And I've been feeling better,' he admitted grudgingly.

'Excellent.' Rebekah beamed at him before walking over to kiss his cheek. 'Now, tell me all about your granddaughter. Is she coming for a visit this Easter?'

'Yes, and she's bringing my very first great-grandchild with her.' Leo beamed and even brought out pictures to show Jake. 'She's only a few months old so I'm a bit nervous about holding her but hold her I will.'

'Great-grandchildren are a rare privilege many people

don't often get to see,' Jake remarked softly. 'You're a very fortunate man, Leo, and I'm sure this little girl…' he indicated the picture Leo held proudly in his hands '…will be the talk of the town.'

'That she will be, mate. That she will be.'

Once they'd finished their tea, they walked out to the car. Leo placed a hand on Rebekah's stomach as she sat in the car.

'Drive safely, young man. You have precious cargo on board.'

'I will.'

'And you, Becky, take care of the town's other baby. A grandchild and great-grandchild to many people around here.'

'Thank you.' Rebekah felt tears gather in her eyes and brushed them away. 'Hormones,' she muttered as she gave Leo a kiss.

'See yer in a few days,' he said, and waved goodbye as Jake reversed out the drive.

'Where's the next stop?'

'One I saved just for you. It's near Angaston so head in that direction and also, if you don't mind, can we stop at a public toilet along the way?'

Jake laughed. 'Might not be a bad idea. I don't think I've had so many cups of tea in one day.'

'I guess you don't get to do a lot of house calls in Sydney.'

At the mention of his home town, the laughter faded. It was as though he'd forgotten where he was and also that he wasn't supposed to be having a good time. She was instantly cross with herself for breaking the jovial mood.

'No. No, I don't.'

'Well, as I said, this next case will definitely interest you.

Amy is twenty-nine weeks pregnant and…well, she's all about your pet topic.'

'FAS?'

'Yes, although she can't see it. She works at her parents' winery, has been around it all her life and has been drinking wine since she was about thirteen. Not excessively then and always under her parents' control.'

'Do they drink?'

'Yes. Again, not excessively but constantly.'

'You think the baby might be in danger?'

'I'm not sure. I only know what I've read in the information published and that's still not conclusive. If we could figure out a way to get Amy to cut down the drinking, it would help. She says she's not drinking as much as before but I'm concerned.'

'Is she married?'

'Yes, but her parents and husband have insisted she quit work for the moment and concentrate on the baby.'

'So they're all out working and she's stuck at home.'

'Yes. I think she might be getting worse at the moment because of picking season and her husband's working longer hours than normal.'

'Has she had much trouble with the pregnancy?'

'A few early alarm bells which is what tipped me off in the first place. I've spoken to the obstetrician about her and he shares my concern but both of us would value your opinion. After all, this is your field of expertise.'

Jake nodded.

'Go left up here.'

He turned the car into a long, rambling driveway which was lined with trees. They were changing colour, some of the leaves already on the ground, and he heard Rebekah sigh. 'You really love this place, don't you?'

'The Barossa? Yes, especially in autumn. It's my favourite season.'

'So you've said.' He brought the car to a halt in the curved gravel drive and came around to help Rebekah out. 'Let's see what we're faced with,' he muttered, after she'd grabbed her medical bag and they'd gone up the stone steps to the front door.

'Dr Sanderson,' Amy said with forced joviality upon opening the door. 'What an unpleasant surprise.'

Rebekah glanced briefly at Jake and then back to their patient. Amy leaned heavily on the door before letting go and staggering slightly away from them. This wasn't good.

'Come to check up on me, no doubt. See that I'm doing the right thing. You shouldn't have worried. I have my husband and my parents *all* checking up on me.' Amy had gone into the living room and sat down on the leather lounge. There was half a glass of wine on the small table in front of her. Rebekah sighed and followed, opening her medical bag and taking out the sphygmomanometer.

'Let me take your blood pressure, Amy.'

'If it'll make you happy,' she slurred, and held out her arm. As Rebekah took her BP, Amy glared at Jake. 'Brought a little friend with you.'

'This is my colleague, Dr Jake Carson. He'll be filling in for me while I'm on maternity leave.'

'No doubt sticking his nose into everyone's business. Giving advice where it's not wanted. That's all you doctors are good for.'

'We're also here to help you,' Rebekah said.

'You sound like my mother.' Amy cleared her throat and mimicked in a nagging voice, '"Call the doctor if you have any pain. Just put your feet up. That's our grandchild you need to look after. Don't do anything."' She growled the last. 'Just lie there all day, be a vegetable and provide nourishment for the baby. Baby, baby, baby. I wish Andrew had never talked me into having this baby.'

'You don't mean that, Amy. It's just the drink talking,' Rebekah soothed. 'BP 170 over 100,' she said to Jake, who only shook his head.

'It is not. I didn't want this child in the first place.'

'How much have you had to drink?' It was the first time Jake had spoken and Amy glared at him.

'Don't you presume to come in here with your high and mighty ways. I don't have to answer any of your questions.'

'How much have you had?' Jake's tone was firmer and more insistent than before.

'How dare you question me?' Amy's voice was becoming shrill.

Jake glanced around the room and then stalked off through a doorway.

'How dare you take such liberties? This isn't your house.' Amy went to stand but it was too difficult. Rebekah put a hand on her shoulder but the other woman shrugged it off. Jake stalked back in with an empty red wine bottle and one that had just been opened.

'Call the ambulance. I want her admitted.'

Rebekah pulled out her mobile phone and made the call.

'You can't do this. You can't just drag me off to hospital.'

'We can if we think either you or the baby is in danger.'

'The baby. There it is again. Ruining my life.'

'Rebekah, pack her some clothes and call her husband,' Jake said, offering his colleague a hand to pull her up.

'Leave Andrew out of this. He has nothing to do with this.' Amy was defiant as Rebekah left the room.

'He is the father of your child. He has a right to know where his wife and child are.'

'I'm staying right here. You can't make me go to hospital

and the baby is fine. It kicked me all last night and the only time it really stops is when I have a glass of wine.' Her words had started out tough but ended on a sob. Jake felt her pain but kept his distance. 'It's ruined my life. I was important before I got pregnant. I helped my father, I ran the business, I was important and now…now I'm just an incubator. They won't let me do anything. They won't let me even look at the paperwork.' Tears started falling but still Jake kept his distance.

He walked over to the hallway where Rebekah had disappeared and called to her. 'Amy needs you,' he said when Rebekah returned. She walked into the room to find Amy sitting on the lounge, rocking slightly backwards and forwards, her hands covering her face as the tears poured out of her. Rebekah rushed over and placed her arm about the other woman and reached into her pocket for a clean handkerchief.

'Here.'

Amy took it, turning slightly in Rebekah's direction and cried. 'You know how hard it is,' Amy wailed.

'Yes, I do.'

'But at least you can keep on working. At least you haven't been told the only thing you're good for is providing for the baby. I can't even blow my nose without them worrying about the baby.'

'I know,' Rebekah soothed. 'They stopped worrying about you, didn't they?' Amy cried harder, letting all the tears and tension out before dozing off.

'Amy.' Rebekah shook the other woman's shoulder. 'The ambulance is here.'

'Huh? Why do I need to go?'

'So we can check that you and the baby are all right. Your blood pressure is higher than it should be.'

'Is that bad?' Amy now looked concerned.

'It might be. Come on,' Rebekah urged. Thankfully, the
fight seemed to have been knocked out of Amy and she
was a compliant patient on the way to the hospital. Jake
and Rebekah drove behind the ambulance and once they
arrived they settled Amy into a room.

Jake filled out the paperwork for the tests he wanted her
to have. 'We'll need to keep you in overnight, which is
why Dr Sanderson packed a bag for you.'

'Yeah, yeah.' Amy closed her eyes. 'Just go away and
let me sleep.'

'Probably a good idea,' Rebekah said as they went out
of the room. Amy needed to sleep off the alcohol and here
she could do it where they could also monitor her condition.
'I'll be around later tonight to check on her,' she told
Monica.

'No. *I'll* be around later tonight,' Jake contradicted.
'Rebekah will be at home, resting.'

Monica nodded in agreement. 'Glad to see *someone* can
make her rest. See you this evening, Dr Carson.'

'What do you need to do now?' he asked as he escorted
Rebekah out of the hospital.

'Fill in the paperwork for the patients we've seen today
and then file them at the surgery.'

'Right. Let's get you back home where you can fill the
paperwork out in comfort and I'll take them over to the
surgery for filing.'

He was being very abrupt. Not relaxed and charming as
he'd been early on during the day. Ever since she'd mentioned his job in Sydney, he'd changed, reverted back to
the man she'd first met on Friday evening. Brisk, efficient
and to the point. She'd thought they'd got past that. At
least, she'd assumed that incredible kiss they'd shared had
taken them past being mere acquaintances.

While they walked over to the house, Rebekah sneaked

a glance at him. His back was ramrod straight; his eyes were focused straight ahead; his stride was purposeful and direct. He was a man with a mission and it appeared that current mission was to get her out of his hair as quickly as possible.

Jake walked directly to the kitchen table and placed the patient files down, ready for her to do. He also brought her bag in and then smiled politely. 'I'll leave you to it, then.'

So that was his current plan—strategic retreat. As he turned and headed back the way he had come, she called his name.

'Need something else? Pickles and strawberries?'

She laughed slightly. 'No. I was just wondering if you'd talk to me.'

He frowned. 'What are we doing, then, if we're not talking?'

'Come on, Jake. You know what I mean. You've reverted to your type-A personality again and although bossing me about might relieve some of your stress, you're still not letting yourself relax completely.'

He raked a hand through his hair and shifted his weight, his gaze locked with hers. 'I don't need lectures from you.'

'I didn't mean for it to be a lecture.' Her words were said softly. 'Come and sit for a few moments and talk to me.' She walked over to the table but didn't sit down.

'What do you want to talk about?' He didn't move.

'Us.'

'Pardon?'

'We can't just pretend that earth-shattering kiss never happened,' she said.

'Why not?'

'Why *not*?' Rebekah was amazed. 'Jake, we *kissed*!'

'I'm well aware of that. What I don't understand is why

we need to discuss it. It happened on the spur of the moment, it will *never* happen again—'

'No need to be so vehement.'

'And it didn't mean anything.' He shrugged with an air of unstudied nonchalance. 'There *is* nothing to talk about.'

'I see. So that's it.'

'Yes.'

Rebekah could feel tears beginning to well up in her eyes and she fought them furiously, silently berating her hormones for making her so overly sensitive.

'You don't want to think about where such an attraction, which does exist between us—I'm not making it up—might end? Come on, Jake. That *kiss*! It was so…' She searched madly for the word to best describe how she'd felt. How she'd been feeling all day long, thanks to that kiss.

'It was so…consuming.' She breathed the last word and closed her eyes momentarily before gazing into his. 'Don't say it was a mistake. Don't say it didn't mean anything.'

'But it didn't.' He took two urgent steps towards her, his tone hard. 'It didn't, Rebekah. It *was* just a kiss. It shouldn't have happened and it will never happen again. You're…you're Guy's widow *and* you're expecting his child. He was a colleague of mine and it hasn't even been a year since he died. I had no business to be kissing you at all. So I apologise profusely and I'd prefer to keep our relationship strictly business.'

'Guy has *nothing* to do with this.'

'Yes, he does.' Jake raked a hand through his hair. 'I respected him as a colleague.'

'And that's great but it has nothing to do with us.'

'There is no ''us''.'

The phone rang and she praised its timing. Glad of the reprieve from fighting emotions which were frantically whirling around within her, Rebekah turned and walked to silence the phone.

'Dr Sanderson.'

'Oh, I'm sorry, dear. I think I might have the wrong number. I was looking for Jake Carson.'

'No, no. You have the right number. I'll just get him for you.' Rebekah turned to face him and held out the receiver. 'It's for you.'

Jake stepped forward and took it from her, their fingers accidentally brushing. Rebekah gasped, her eyes wide with repressed emotion. Their gazes held for that split second and she thought she glimpsed a softening in his blue depths but it vanished almost immediately. She turned and left him to his call.

'Hello?'

'Who was that?' his mother asked.

'Rebekah.'

'Is she the one who's pregnant?'

'Yes.'

'What's she doing there?'

'She lives here.'

There was silence on the other end of the phone. 'You're sharing a house with your colleague? You didn't mention this before.'

'Is there a problem with that?' His tone was a little harsh. What was it with women and questions? 'Sorry.' He exhaled harshly. 'It's been a busy day.'

'Not too stressful, I hope.'

'Nothing like Sydney.'

'And so Rebekah—is she nice?'

Jake closed his eyes, knowing he wasn't going to get any peace until all her questions had been answered. 'Yes.'

'Is she the one who's pregnant?'

'Yes.'

'You're tired.'

'Yes.'

'All right. I won't keep you, then. Dad's doing fine but I'm sure you knew that as the doctor told me he'd spoken to you. We're at home now but I'll call you soon. Go and rest, darling. I worry about you.'

'I know.' Once he'd rung off, he turned and looked towards Rebekah's end of the house. He felt like a heel. He knew what he'd said earlier had upset her and it was the last thing he'd wanted to do. He also hadn't wanted to discuss his loss of clarity and sense when he'd kissed her earlier that day.

Following his common sense, he turned away, picked up the patient files from the table and headed into his bedroom. He needed to keep his distance from Rebekah, now more than ever. Getting involved with her was not the smart thing to do—neither would it help decrease his stress levels.

Jake put the work on the table and lay down on his bed for a moment. Lacing his hands behind his head, he closed his eyes and took a deep breath. The memory of his lips on hers was far too vivid. The scent of her, the feel of her, the taste of her. They were a heady combination and one he reluctantly admitted he wanted more of.

It was wrong, though. This craving he had for her went against all his morals, his ethics and his common sense.

Yet there were some things in life that didn't make any sense—and his need for Rebekah Sanderson appeared to be one of them.

CHAPTER SIX

'THIS is the third time you've been here in under a week, Becky,' Gillian said softly as she sat down next to her friend.

'I just want to catch up regarding the patients. I tend to sleep a lot at the moment, especially during the day, because at night-time the baby thinks it's time to play.'

'A sign of things to come.' Gillian laughed.

'I sincerely hope not,' Rebekah retorted, and rubbed her ever-increasing stomach. 'Uh,' she sighed. 'I can't believe how unsettled my life is. Just when I think I have it right, something drastic happens and my life comes tumbling down in a heap once more.' She glared at her stomach. 'When are you going to arrive?'

Gillian laughed at her impatience. 'The baby will be born on its birthday.'

'Yeah, but when's *that* going to be? I'm thirty-eight weeks and I don't think I want to hang around much longer in this state.'

'How was Amy when you saw her today?'

Rebekah made the so-so gesture with her hand. 'She's not drinking, at least—not that she's admitting but she's very depressed. Those two nights she spent in hospital a couple of weeks ago made her realise that this is very serious. I would also say that she hasn't received a lot of support from her husband or her parents. They really do seem more concerned about the baby than her.' Rebekah shook her head.

'Should they get counselling?'

'I've recommended it and left the number of a good therapist with Amy.' Rebekah shrugged.

'What about Jake? What does he think of the situation?'

'He said it doesn't look good. Amy may still miscarry at any stage. If she doesn't, the likelihood that the baby will be born with some sort of deformity has rapidly increased and even then he can't say whether or not the baby will live.'

'Does Amy know this?'

'He's told her the facts.'

Gillian nodded. 'Would you like another glass of milk?'

'No. I'm fine.' Rebekah glanced at the clock on the wall. 'Nine-thirty. I guess I should be getting home.' She made no move.

'Why are you avoiding him so much?'

'What? Who?'

'Jake.' Gillian's tone was sympathetic yet knowing.

'Oh, Gillian.' Rebekah covered her face with her hands and sighed. 'He's so nice and wonderful and caring and I can't help it but I really like him.'

Gillian clapped her hands with glee as Rebekah looked at her. 'What's the problem, then?'

'You don't see it? The problem is—how can I trust him? You're right that I've been avoiding him but I know he's been avoiding me as well. He told me he didn't want to get involved with me because I was Guy's wife but the truth is that I don't know if I *want* to get involved with anyone right now. I mean, my life has dramatically changed during the last twelve months, I'm about to have a baby and I think that's about all the change I can handle for the time being.'

'But...?' Gillian prompted.

'But I really like him.' She closed her eyes and whimpered. 'I don't want to. I don't want to be attracted to him but I am. I find myself wanting to get inside his head, to get to know him really well, to be with him, to touch him. Then I start to question his motives. What does *he* want? Am I just a passing fancy while he's here in Tanunda? Someone to be forgotten when he leaves? If something big does happen between us, will he go back to Sydney for a holiday and hook up with an old girlfriend? I just don't know if I can trust him, Gillian.'

'You don't know him well enough.'

'But that's just the thing—I feel as though I know him really well. It's as though we've connected on some unconscious level and I've never felt anything like that before. Not even with Guy.'

'Guy was different. *You* were different back then to what you are now. You drifted into the relationship with Guy because he was the first man who'd shown you affection. Your parents had starved you so much, you were like a child in a candy store when Guy came around. Then, over the years, you both settled into a comfortable routine. There was no thunder, no lightning, no spark—just the day-to-day routine.'

'Do you think *that's* why Guy…did what he did?'

'Possibly, but you must realise that it didn't have anything to do with *you*. The fact that Jake wants to hold back *because* you were married to a colleague of his is an admirable quality, Becky. It shows he has morals and ethics and he's willing to live by them. Now, that's a sure-fire sign that perhaps here is a man you can trust. But, hey, I could be wrong. Don't go doing anything just on my say-so.'

Rebekah didn't say anything but knew Gillian was watching her thoughtfully.

'I think there's more to this story than you're telling me.'

'Yes,' Rebekah admitted. 'You're right.' She looked

down at her hands and studied her nails. 'Two weeks ago, I couldn't sleep. I was emotional—as per usual—'

'It's common for your hormones to run wild.'

'Wild enough to kiss the man?'

'Oh, Rebekah, you didn't.' Gillian covered her mouth in surprised delight.

'Actually, I think it was he who kissed me. Anyway, regardless of who started it, we kissed and then that night he tells me that the kiss meant nothing, that it will never happen again and that he was sorry. I was Guy's wife, so I'm off limits.'

'Why do they always have to apologise for kissing?'

'I know.' Rebekah threw her hands up in the air. 'What is it with men? I wanted the kiss, he wanted the kiss—otherwise we wouldn't have kissed in the first place.'

'Was it good?'

Rebekah's eyes flashed with remembered desire and she nodded eagerly. 'Was it ever! There is definitely… something…between us but at the moment I can't see it going anywhere.' She sighed and shook her head. 'See what I mean about my life just tumbling into a heap again? Here I am on the brink of having my baby and all I can think about is Jake Carson. I mean, what man in his right mind would be attracted to me? Look at me! I'm huge!'

'You're pregnant.' Gillian corrected. 'And you're all baby. You've watched your weight carefully and have hardly put any extra on. Once the baby is born and you're back to your normal size, you'll feel better.'

'I know. It's all silly, it's all emotional but…' She sighed. 'It was *so* nice to think that he might be attracted to me, especially when I'm huge like this. Do you have any idea what that did for my self-esteem?'

'I can imagine.'

'And then he apologises and tells me it was just a kiss and it didn't mean anything. Can you imagine how that felt?'

'Humiliating?'

'Got it in one. Since then we've kept our distance. He's up and out of the house early in the morning and I've taken to visiting people in the evening to give him some time to work, instead of hibernating in my bedroom.'

'That's very considerate of you.'

'If I didn't, then he'd probably go out and he's got nowhere to go.'

'True. Or here's a thought—you could just try talking to him.'

'I do talk to him but there's only so much we can say about our patients. He didn't do house calls with me today.'

'How did you manage, driving by yourself?'

'Fine, although uncomfortable. But it's OK. My back's pretty sore tonight. More so than usual.'

'Put a wheat bag on it at bedtime.'

'Yes, Mum.'

'And here's some more advice—stop worrying about him. Once the baby is born, you'll feel better. Your life will settle down into a nice, easy rhythm and Jake Carson will return to Sydney and all will be forgotten.'

'It could be my hormones that are telling me I'm attracted to him when I'm really not.' She closed her eyes and shook her head. 'Man, that sounds silly when I say it out loud.'

'But why don't we blame those troublesome hormones at the moment?'

'Yes. Yes, I think you're right.'

'And after all, he's the only good-looking, single man of your age in the vicinity.'

'True. Very true.'

'So there you go. Opportunity and motive, all of which you had absolutely no control over. You are not to blame.'

'Excellent.' Rebekah shifted out of the chair and stood. 'Thanks, Gillian. I'm glad I came over tonight.'

'So am I. Go home, have a snack, get a wheat bag warmed up and lie down with a good book.'

'Sounds like the perfect prescription. I'll just use your bathroom first.'

Jake stared out the window at the dark and empty street. There weren't as many streetlights here as there were surrounding his apartment in Sydney. The night sky seemed darker, the stars seemed brighter and he could swear there were more stars here than there were in Sydney.

Where was Rebekah?

He turned from the window, paced around the room before hearing a faint noise and returning to look out the window. No. That wasn't her.

He raked a hand through his hair, feeling guilty about driving her out of her own home. He knew she left because of him. He felt it. If she stayed home, she would hibernate in her bedroom and when she got up for her usual three am snacks, he made sure he stayed put.

Two weeks ago, he'd told her the kiss they'd shared had meant nothing. Since then, if she went out in the evenings, he found it almost impossible to work until she was safe at home. He was conscious of her whenever she walked into the house, regardless of whether or not he was in the same room. At the surgery, during practice meetings, during house calls. It didn't matter where she was, he *felt* her and it was driving him insane.

Where was she? He stared out the window and when a set of headlights flashed as they turned into the driveway his whole body relaxed with relief.

Quickly he walked into the kitchen and opened the refrigerator. He poured himself a drink of water and was about to return to his room when the phone rang. Rebekah walked in at the same time and as she was closer, she picked up the receiver.

'Dr Sanderson.'

'Hello, Becky.'

'Oh, hi, Mrs Carson.'

'I've told you before, call me Deliah,' she insisted, and Rebekah smiled. The two of them had chatted a few times during the past couple of weeks, especially if she called when Jake wasn't around.

'I'll try.' Jake was standing in the middle of the kitchen, glass of water in hand. 'Jake's here so I'll put him on.'

'Before you do, how are you feeling?'

'Not bad. Tired, of course, but nothing out of the ordinary.'

'I remember it well. The memory never really goes.'

'How's your husband?'

'Progressing nicely, dear. Thank you for asking.'

'Here's Jake,' Rebekah said, and handed the receiver over, ensuring their fingers didn't touch. She also held her breath, hoping she wouldn't have to breathe in the alluring scent of him. Hurrying from the room, she quickly disappeared behind her bedroom door.

She liked his mother, she admitted begrudgingly. She liked *him*. Regardless of the silly, mind-game rubbish she and Gillian had just been discussing, Rebekah knew without a doubt that the longer Jake stayed around, the stronger her feelings became.

Gillian was right. He was different from Guy. He had morals, ethics and she'd seen that in his work life as well. He was understanding and sympathetic with his patients, as well as firm when the need arose.

Eight days ago, Jake had called her at home and asked her to come over to the clinic. Myron, a little boy with autism, had come in for a check-up. He hadn't been sleeping or eating well due to a major upheaval in his life. Then, to be faced with a different doctor, the little boy had gone into 'shut-down' mode.

When he'd seen Rebekah, he'd brightened somewhat but he'd still been uninterested in everything that had been going on. She'd watched as Jake had woven his magic around the boy, asking him questions—specific questions—designed to get information from the nine-year-old.

Myron's mother and Rebekah were stupefied at the outcome. Then again, she'd had to remind herself that he was a paediatrician and that this sort of thing would be second nature to him. Still, he had been impressive—and compassionate. Something her husband hadn't been.

Guy had often cancelled clinics, dumping the extra load onto Gillian and herself just so he could pursue his sailing hobby. Of course, with three doctors in the practice, they'd been able to cope but, still, it hadn't been the professional thing to do. Funny—she started to pace—she'd never really considered just how much extra work Guy had made for her. She hadn't complained, she'd just carried on—at work and at home—pretending she was happy.

'Ah, hindsight,' she said to the baby, and then stopped still as a sharp spasm gripped her lower abdomen. Rebekah gasped in shock. The pain stayed for a moment or two and then went away. 'Ow.' She rubbed the area where the pain had been before crossing to her desk. She opened the bag of bread she kept on her desk, before spreading some chocolate spread on it. It had been easier for her to keep a stash of food in her room, rather than risk waking Jake when she needed an early morning snack. She had wanted no more early morning meetings in case her hormones acted up again and grabbed the man for another heart-wrenching kiss.

Rebekah sat down on the chair and felt instant discomfort, which made her opt for standing. She munched on the sandwich, trying not to think about the man in the other room. There, that should take care of the baby for a while. Right now she should start getting ready for bed and heat up the wheat bag. As she walked to her *en suite*, another spasm hit.

It was then she felt a loosening sensation before a trickle of water slid down her leg. Her eyes widened in alarm as she rushed to the bathroom and stepped into the shower.

'What?' She wasn't sure what to do so she just stood there, waiting for the liquid to stop running down her legs. 'Oh, my gosh,' she whispered. 'This is it.'

Trembling, she thumped on the wall. 'Jake! Jake!' She waited, not knowing whether he was off the phone or not. If he was down in his bedroom, he might not hear her. The flow of amniotic fluid was slowing down and she started to relax a little. 'Jake!' she called again, and thumped on the wall, concern in her tone.

'Rebekah?'

She breathed a sigh of relief. He'd heard her. 'Jake.' He knocked on her bedroom door, which she thought was cute. 'Come in. Come in. I'm in the bathroom.' A moment later, he stood in the doorway.

'What's wrong? Why are you standing in the shower fully clothed?'

'My waters…' She broke off on a gasp as another spasm hit. She closed her eyes and clenched her teeth.

'You're in labour? But you still have two weeks to go.'

She would have laughed, if she'd been able to. As it was, she concentrated on the pain which seemed to be getting stronger as well as longer. Finally, it subsided and she relaxed against the shower wall, opening her eyes to look at him.

'I'll call the hospital and, uh…let them know we'll be over soon.' He reached out a hand to her but thought better of it and let it fall helplessly back to his side. 'Has it stopped?'

'Yes.'

He pressed some buttons on his watch. 'Let's see how far apart they are. I'll be back as quickly as I can.' He stalked out of the room, feeling far from comfortable and far from controlled. He picked up the receiver from where he'd left it. 'Rebekah's just started labour. I have to go,' he told his mother.

'Oh, my word. Go, dear. Go and be supportive for her. She's got no one else, Jake.'

He wanted to dispute the fact, to say she had the entire town there waiting to help her, but now wasn't the time to get into a discussion with his mother.

'Call me later.'

'I will.' He hung up and quickly called the hospital. 'Rebekah's in labour. I'm timing the contractions, we'll be over there shortly.' He waited for confirmation of his words before disconnecting the call and hurrying back to her side. 'Has the next contraction started?'

'No.' She gritted her teeth as the pain returned. 'Yes.'

'Just over three minutes.' Jake waited for her to relax, wishing there was something he could do to help. 'Settling down yet?'

She glared at him.

'Ah…I'll take that as a no.' He waited until the contraction ended, starting his watch again. 'I'll help you through the house and into the car.'

'No car. Can't sit down. I'll walk.'

'You want to walk to the hospital?'

'It's not far.'

'I don't know if it's a good idea.'

'Then I'll be having it here because I can't sit down!' she shouted.

'All right. Sure. We'll walk.' He held out his hand to her and when she didn't take it he levelled her with a warning glare. 'Accept my help, Rebekah. I want to give it and, more importantly, you need it.'

'Fine.'

Jake laughed at her grudging surrender, the rich sound washing over her in waves of happiness. How was it possible that she could feel so happy and so annoyed with him at the same time? She knew the thought wasn't worth dwelling on so placed her hand in his as he helped her from the shower.

'I know you'd probably feel better if you change but let's get you over the road first. Someone can come back for clothes and things like that later.'

'My bag is packed,' she said, and motioned to the small suitcase by her bed. 'Just pick it up.'

'I'll get it later. I think I'd like to concentrate on getting one package at a time over to the hospital.'

'Gee, thanks. I'm a package now, am I?' Reluctantly, she smiled at him, feeling a little better.

He chuckled. 'Good to see you smiling.' They went slowly, taking small but steady steps, out the front door and across the lawn. They'd just crossed the road when the next contraction hit.

'Right on time,' Jake announced. Rebekah gripped his arm tightly as she closed her eyes and concentrated through the pain. Neither of them moved until it was over. 'The duration is getting longer.'

'Tell me about it.'

Jake let go of her hand and flexed his fingers. 'Just getting the blood flowing again, ready for the next time.'

Rebekah laughed. 'Thanks.'

'Hey, no problem.' He placed his right arm around her back and held her hand with his left. 'The ground's a bit uneven here.' They started off again, little baby steps, slowly getting closer to the hospital. Not far from the front door she gripped his hand and leaned in closer. Jake rubbed her back with his other hand, hoping it did something to bring her relief. He felt so utterly helpless and wasn't really sure what he should or shouldn't be doing but as she wasn't yelling at him, he took this as a good sign.

The night CNC came rushing out with a wheelchair. Jake shook his head. 'Rebekah prefers to walk.'

'I don't *prefer* it,' she snapped as the contraction eased. 'I *can't* sit down.'

'Walking will help speed up the labour,' the sister said.

'I think it's moving along pretty fast all by itself. My first contraction was about fifteen minutes ago.'

'Good. Gillian's on her way. Let's get you inside and see what's happening.'

They made a stop-start procession up the corridor with Rebekah having another contraction in the middle. She leaned her head against Jake's shoulder and he rubbed her back soothingly. When it had passed, the sister led her into the labour ward. The bed had a floral, frilly spread on it with several throw cushions making it seem more homely.

Rebekah had delivered several babies in this room, had walked passed it several times and had always thought it looked very pretty. Now—she wanted to hurl the cushions at the window and rake the feminine cover from the bed. She was in pain and the last thing she wanted was pretty, relaxing things around her. Where were the drugs?

Oh, it was wonderful that Gillian was on her way, that

Jake and the night CNC were being ever so attentive, but where was the anaesthetist? He was the one who could give her some pain relief, an epidural—anything.

'Colin. Ring Colin,' she said.

'I've already called him. He's on his way.'

Rebekah glared the sister. 'Go and get him *now*.'

'I'll settle her in,' Jake remarked, noticing the surprised look on the sister's face.

'I don't need *anyone* to settle me,' Rebekah added. 'I'm fine. Women have babies all the time and now it's my turn and I'm *fine*!'

'Yes, you are,' Jake pacified her as he tossed the cushions off the bed onto a chair and pulled the bedspread back. Rebekah smirked in a self-satisfied way at the inanimate objects, glad of his rough treatment of them. He wound the bed down so it was easier for her to get on but she found she couldn't.

'Can't lie down either.' She looked at him, her eyes beginning to fill with tears. 'I can't sit down, I can't lie down and my legs are aching and tired.'

'I know. I know,' he soothed. 'Lean on me.' He gathered her near so her head was resting on his shoulder.

'I'm sorry if I'm being horrible.'

'You're not,' he soothed.

'Liar.'

'Probably.'

She pulled back to look at him, her terrified gaze meeting his sympathetic blue one. 'Thank you,' she whispered.

Jake felt a knot of tension, need and anger churn in his gut. Tension, because he was fighting as hard as he could against the attraction. Need, because it was becoming impossible *not* to give in and kiss her—and anger, because he had no self-control where she was concerned.

She was an amazing woman and his feelings for her were

intensifying with every moment he spent in her company. It wasn't right. He knew that but he also knew the wrong thing could sometimes feel so right.

Jake swallowed all his thoughts and emotions and bent down to kiss her forehead. 'You'll be fine.' He felt her tense and knew another contraction was on the way. He helped her through it, his eyes closed as they leaned against each other, both concentrating on what was happening. When he opened his eyes, it was to find Gillian standing in the doorway, watching them.

'Good evening. You look as though you're having loads of fun.' She came in and patted Rebekah lightly on the shoulder. 'So, this back pain you told me about earlier tonight. Guess what that was about? Has anyone checked the baby?'

Jake waited for Rebekah to answer but when she didn't, he shook his head.

'Can you get up on the bed?'

'Too uncomfortable,' she mumbled.

'OK. Stay where you are, I'll work around you.' For the next ten minutes, there were people in and out of the room, the baby's heartbeat was checked and found to be perfect. Rebekah was given the once-over by Gillian and pronounced to be 'moving along nicely'.

When Colin arrived, she was having a contraction and in the middle of it she started to push.

'Was that a push?' Gillian asked. They all waited and when Rebekah pushed again, Colin chuckled.

'Well, you don't need me now,' he joked.

'Yes. Yes, I do.' Rebekah grabbed him by the front of his shirt and dragged his face closer. 'Give me something. Anything!'

'I can't, Becky. You know that.'

'The window has closed?' she asked incredulously.

'The window has closed,' he confirmed.

'Open a door,' she whimpered.

'Becky.' Colin passed a comforting hand over her fore-head. 'You'll be fine. The baby's fine. There seems to be an abundance of people in here so I'll be in the kitchen if you need me.'

Rebekah reached out a hand but he was gone. Her window was shut and so was the door. Why couldn't he open it again? She stuck out her lower lip. 'I don't want to do this any more.'

Gillian laughed. 'You're doing a great job and the fact that you're saying you want to go home proves that everything is moving along nicely.' When the next contraction gripped, Rebekah pushed again. She rested her head on Jake's shoulder between contractions and closed her eyes, conserving what energy she had.

It seemed to take for ever but an hour later Gillian told her to give one more push and the head was finally out. The cord wasn't around the neck and they waited while the shoulders rotated. She'd managed to get comfortable on a beanbag as her legs had eventually given up supporting her.

Jake held her hand tightly, dabbing her forehead with a damp cloth. She hadn't wanted him to go and he'd made no move to leave. Now they were almost finished and she could hardly believe the man she'd known for only a few weeks had stayed to help her through.

Rebekah knew it was ridiculous but…she loved him. She knew hardly anything about him but, still, she loved him. Perhaps it was the hormones or the intimacy of their present situation but her feelings would not be repressed. She closed her eyes and rested her head back. What a revelation to have at such a time!

The next contraction started to grip and she squeezed his hand once more.

'That's it. Good girl. Keep going, Becky,' Gillian coached. 'Snatch a breath—one more push and…'

Rebekah felt the baby leave her and was amazed at the sense of loss. The intimacy only *she* could share with her child was over. Everything was silent for a second or two and she didn't even realise that Jake had let go of her hand to quickly assist Gillian—and then it came. The most glorious sound in the entire world—the cry of a newborn babe.

Gillian placed the child into Rebekah's waiting arms. 'You have a daughter.'

The loss she'd just felt vanished into thin air as she held her little girl for the very first time, kissing the soft, downy head.

'Oh, baby.' Her eyes filled with tears which spilled over. 'Baby, you're here.'

'What are you going to call her?' The question came from Jake, his voice not quite so steady. Rebekah looked up to see his own eyes glistening with tears. She reached out a hand to him which he took, drawing him closer.

'Jake…' Her throat was scratchy and sore and with the swell of emotion she felt it was no wonder it was hard to speak.

'Really? I think you can think of a prettier name than that,' he whispered.

She laughed and swallowed. 'Will you help me?'

'Name her?' When she nodded he smiled. 'I'd be delighted.'

The child in her arms slept, their gazes held and slowly but surely he moved in closer. The kiss he pressed on her lips was the most natural thing he'd ever done. The feeling of coming home was the most natural feeling he'd ever felt.

And he was at a loss to explain why neither terrified him.

CHAPTER SEVEN

'HERE'S another list of names,' Gillian said as she came for her morning round.

'Thanks.' Rebekah sat in bed, propped up by pillows, feeding her beautiful daughter.

'I can't believe she's two days old and you still haven't thought of a name.'

'I want to find one that suits her. I like Susan Isabella but then her initials would be SIS.'

Gillian perched herself on the end of the bed. 'You're not going to give her Guy's surname?'

'You seem surprised.'

'No. No, just…hadn't really thought that far.'

Rebekah looked down at her little girl and sadly shook her head. 'Even if Guy were here, he wouldn't have been interested in a child.'

'Too selfish.' Gillian nodded. 'What about Guy's parents?'

'They haven't been interested in the baby so far. I'll notify them in a few weeks when things have settled down. I guess we'll see what happens then.'

Gillian nodded again. 'Has Jake been in this morning?'

'Not yet but we're expecting him soon.' The baby had finished feeding and Rebekah sat her up to burp her. 'Aren't we beautiful? We're expecting Jake really soon. Yes, we are. Oh, you're so precious.'

'So the two of you—you and Jake, I mean—seem to be getting along well at the moment. Definitely not avoiding each other.'

'No. It's like we've called some sort of…truce but nothing's actually been said. It's nice.'

Gillian looked at her closely. 'Be careful, Becky.'

'Careful about what?'

'About falling in love with the guy.'

'I think your warning might be too late.'

'Oh, you haven't…have you?'

'Yes, I think I have.'

'Becky!'

'I know, I know. I didn't ask for this to happen but it has.'

'When? I mean when did you realise this?'

'During labour.'

'Oh.' Gillian physically relaxed. 'Oh, well, that doesn't count, then. The whole birthing process is driven by hormones.'

'It's not the hormones, Gillian.' Rebekah was serious. 'It's the real thing.'

'Sure about that?'

'Yes.'

'And what are you going to do about it?'

'I…I don't know. I honestly don't know.' She was in a flap. 'I just turn to mush when I see him and I love the way he smells and he's so caring and gentle. I've never felt this way before.'

'Not even with Guy?'

'No. Not even with Guy. This is…different and it's really scaring me.'

'Hmm.' Gillian frowned again. 'Perhaps it *is* the real thing. What about Jake? How does he feel?'

'I don't know.'

'You haven't talked?'

'I've…er…been a little preoccupied since I realised my

feelings,' Rebekah pointed out, rubbing her cheek against the baby's head.

'I must say, I was surprised when he kissed you after the birth,' Gillian said. 'And it wasn't just a quick peck on the lips.'

'No.'

'No. It looked to be a full-blown, lips pressed firmly to yours, passion-and-fire-stoking kiss.'

'I remember it well and he hasn't even apologised for it.'

Both women sighed, then laughed. Rebekah rewrapped her daughter in a blanket. 'I like Elizabeth. Are you an Elizabeth?'

'Elizabeth?' Jake said as he strode into the room. 'Elizabeth Sanderson. Has a ring to it. I gather you've given up Susan?'

'Yes. I don't think she looks like a Susan any more.'

'What about…Anabella?' he said softly.

Rebekah watched as he scooped the baby up into his arms as though it were the most natural thing in the world. He kissed her head.

'Anabella. Anabella Sanderson.' She mulled it over. 'I quite like it. Anabella. Does she look like an Anabella, Jake?'

He studied the little girl who was going to sleep in his arms. 'You know, I think she does.'

'What about a middle name?' Gillian suggested.

'Where did you get Anabella from?' Rebekah didn't want it to be from one of his old girlfriends.

'It was my great-grandmother's name.'

'It's very pretty.' Gillian raised her eyebrows at Rebekah, as though to say, What do you think about that, then?

'We need something that goes with Anabella,' Jake continued, rocking gently from side to side.

They all thought. 'What about Janice?' Gillian asked.

'No.'

'Rebekah?' Jake suggested.

'Anabella Rebekah—no, too many ''b's'',' Rebekah replied.

'But she deserves to carry your name,' he continued. 'You did an amazing job bringing her into this world.'

'Thank you but no.' She looked at her daughter— Anabella—being held by the man she loved. Jake. Jake Carson. 'What about…Jane?'

'Jane.' He nodded, consideringly.

'Jane,' Gillian echoed.

'Anabella is kind of a fancy name and Jane settles it down, if you know what I mean.'

'They blend.' Jake smiled.

'Exactly. Anabella Jane Sanderson.'

'It's pretty,' Gillian remarked. She looked from one to the other. 'Decided?'

Rebekah smiled at Jake. 'Decided. Anabella Jane she is.'

'This calls for a celebration,' Gillian said, and headed off to tell the rest of the staff.

'Is she asleep?'

'Yes.'

'Did you want to put her down?'

'No.' He smiled sheepishly. 'I like holding her.'

'Me, too.'

'So how are you feeling today?'

'Good. We both had a good four-hour stretch of solid sleep this morning.'

'You could do with a bit more.'

'Look like a hag, do I?'

He smiled teasingly. 'I didn't say that.'

'No, but you implied it.'

'Rebekah, I would never imply that you looked like a hag. A little sleep-deprived, yes, but a hag? Never.'

She laughed. 'Smooth talker. You watch him, Anabella, and don't let him get away with anything.'

Jake sat on the bed near her and angled Anabella up in his arms so they could both look at her sleeping face. 'She's beautiful, Bek.'

At the nickname, Rebekah caught her breath. She was having a hard time coping with his nearness as well as deciphering the looks he was giving her. His blue eyes were filled with promise and desire—and she wasn't sure what she wanted to believe the most.

'She is.' The words were whispered with sincere emotion and Rebekah felt her love for him increase tenfold in that one second. She'd never thought it possible before, to love a man as she did Jake, but here she was. Living proof!

Their gazes met and held. The atmosphere in the room intensified. Her lips parted, her breathing increasing as the moment stretched on.

It was the perfect opportunity for him to kiss her again. To place his lips on hers in the loving way he'd done two days ago, kissing her until she swooned due to lack of oxygen. He was so mind-numbingly good at it, she was impatient for them to get started.

He leaned in a little closer and she could feel his breath, mingling with hers. He shifted slightly and cleared his throat.

'I've been told you want to discharge yourself tomorrow.'

The moment vanished but he didn't move away.

'Yes. I'd like to get home and settled into a routine. I'm not far from the hospital, both you and Gillian will be across the road at the clinic during the day should we need anything and you'll be in the house in the evenings. I don't see any reason to stay.'

'I'm not criticising you, I'm merely making a statement. The reason I made the statement is that I was also told about the hospital's custom.'

'Custom?'

'Well, it can't be a very good one if their own GP doesn't know about it.'

'Which one?' she asked cautiously.

'The one where the new mother is taken out to dinner for a few hours the night before she returns home. A celebration for her hard labour.' He raised his eyebrows on the pun.

Rebekah felt tingles of excitement buzz through her. She nodded, wanting desperately to hear what he said next and all the while wanting to hold onto the moment for as long as she could. 'What did you have in mind?' She prayed fervently that he wasn't suggesting a night out with the girls and that he would stay and keep an eye on Anabella.

'Dinner.'

'Dinner,' she repeated.

'With me.'

Yes! 'Uh…where were you thinking of going?'

'I hadn't actually thought that far but I'll make a reservation today.' His beeper sounded. 'That'll be Nicole, making sure I'm not late for clinic. I guess I have to go.' Reluctantly, Jake handed her the baby, their arms and hands touching briefly—but it was enough for them both to stop, stare at each other, before mumbling muffled apologies. 'Enjoy your steady stream of visitors,' he remarked, trying to break the tension.

'We will. They'll all be even more thrilled now that she has a name.'

'Some will be disappointed, I think. The ladies at the

information centre in town had started a competition to see if anyone could guess the name.'

'Well, I hope you didn't enter.'

'They wouldn't let me.' He grinned. 'See you at seven tonight.' With one last, heart-melting smile, he left.

'And then there were two.' Rebekah shuffled down in the bed, discarding pillows as she went until finally she and Anabella were snuggled up together. 'I love you, Anabella,' she whispered and kissed the downy forehead. 'And I love the man who chose your name.'

'Knock, knock.'

Rebekah opened her eyes and smiled at Hetty.

'I didn't want to wake you, dear, but Sister said it was all right to come in.'

Rebekah shifted up on the pillows. 'It's fine. I was just resting my eyes. Anabella and I had a big sleep earlier this morning.'

'Anabella! That's a beautiful name.'

'For a beautiful girl.' Rebekah looked down at the sleeping baby in her arms. 'Would you like a cuddle?'

'Do you need to ask?' Hetty put her bag down and held out her arms. 'Oh, Rebekah, dear, she's perfect. Look at her little fingers peeking over the top of her blanket.'

'Yes. She is quite…perfect.' Rebekah sighed lovingly. The afternoon tea was brought around and Hetty agreed to join her.

'I've dropped some food in for you. I had to leave it with Nicole at the clinic because when I went to sneak in the back door to your house it was locked.'

'Jake.' Rebekah nodded and then smiled. 'He's still used to the city lifestyle. Anyway, thank you for the food.'

'My pleasure. Have you had many visitors today?'

'Not too many. Monica is limiting my intake.'

Hetty laughed. 'Not surprising. Everyone wants to see the new addition to our town.'

'Yes, they do. I'm glad you've dropped in today. I was starting to worry about you.'

'Don't worry about me, dear. I'm fine. I saw your Dr Carson yesterday and my blood pressure is normal and the treatment for my stomach ulcer is working a treat.'

'He's not *my* Dr Carson, Hetty.'

'Really?' Hetty raised her eyebrows in surprise. 'OK. We'll play it your way for now.' Anabella started to stir and Hetty handed her back. No sooner were Anabella's eyes open than she began to cry.

'Oh, baby. Are you hungry?' The little wails continued and Rebekah unbuttoned her top, wincing slightly as Anabella found what she was looking for. 'Oh, that first bit is painful.' Slowly she relaxed.

'I like Jake Carson, Becky, as, I might add, does most of the town.'

'And?'

'And I think you should go for it.'

'Go for it? Meaning?'

'Take another chance. It's not easy, let me tell you. Clive is my second husband.'

'Really?' Rebekah was astonished. 'Why didn't I know that?'

'Because it happened a very long time ago. I was, like you, widowed at a young age. My first marriage wasn't particularly a happy one but we got by. It wasn't until later, when I met Clive, that I realised what true love was. Everything was different. The stars were brighter, the breeze was lighter. Clive let me be myself and urged me to do the things I wanted. Clive had no great ambition in life—other than to help people, which he does. He was more than happy for me to be the main breadwinner and back then that was a big thing for a man to do.'

Anabella had finished feeding and Hetty held out her hands so she could burp her. 'Jake's a good man, Becky. You know, as well as I do, that when he returns to Sydney, he'll get all stressed out again and be right back where he started. Slowing down for a while is good but changing your lifestyle permanently so you live at a slower pace is going to be difficult for him. You need him and he needs you.'

'I don't know about that.'

Hetty rocked the sleeping baby in her arms. 'We need him here—in the valley. You're going to need help raising this little girl.'

'I have my town-family to help do that.'

'I know, dear…but it's not the same.'

'Right now I don't know if I'm capable of making life changing decisions. I need to concentrate on Anabella and myself. We need to find out who we are together before we can let anyone else into our lives. Maybe…in time.'

Rebekah shook her head, her mind in a whirl. 'I appreciate what you've said, though. Thanks.'

'Yoo-hoo!' Sylvia and Margaret came into the room and when they saw the sleeping baby they started to whisper. 'Hello, Hetty. Nice to see you. Ooh, look at the little darling. I think she's grown since yesterday. Has she been feeding well, Dr Sanderson? Look, we've made her a little outfit. Don't you think she'll look as pretty as a picture in it?'

Hetty handed over the sleeping baby to Margaret and kissed Rebekah on the cheek. 'Take care.'

'Thanks, Hetty.'

'How did she sleep last night?' Margaret asked, cooing

over the sleeping child. Rebekah sighed, her mind switching down a gear before she smiled at her new visitors and answered their questions.

'No dinner for you tonight.' Gillian waltzed into Rebekah's room, carrying a garment bag.

'Pardon?' For one heart-stopping moment Rebekah thought Jake had cancelled.

'From the hospital kitchen, I mean.'

'Whew!' She placed her hand over her heart. 'Don't *do* that to me.'

Gillian laughed. 'Sorry. Here. I brought you a surprise.' She held out the garment bag. 'It's my present to you.'

Rebekah unzipped the bag and gasped as she took out a breathtaking black dress. It was simple, elegant and one that she'd admired in an Adelaide boutique for months. She looked from the dress to Gillian. 'How did you do it?'

'I had a friend buy it and express post it to me.'

'Oh, Gillian.' Rebekah could feel the tears brimming in her eyes. She put the dress on the bed and rushed to hug her friend. 'Thank you. Thank you so much.'

Rebekah smiled as she picked up the dress and held it against her before turning to Anabella who was sleeping in the hospital cot. 'Look, princess. Does Mummy look pretty?'

'Mummy looks sickeningly good,' Gillian said. 'I wish my figure had come back as quickly as yours. I don't know. You have an easy and quick labour and a few days later you're almost back to what you were before you became pregnant. It's just not fair.'

Rebekah laughed. 'I can't help it.'

'No. Although I would like to add that when you get pregnant again—some time in the future—we keep a close eye on you when you go into labour because, boy, oh, boy, do you go quickly. You'll be lucky to make it across the road to the hospital with the next one.'

'What *next one*?' she scoffed, but didn't dwell on it. 'I want to enjoy the baby I have because if I blink, she'll be on her way to university.'

Gillian laughed. 'Too true. All right. Jake's going to be here soon so let's get you organised.' She pulled out a large sponge-bag with cosmetics, a hairdryer, curlers and hair spray, as well as a pair of stockings. 'I stopped by your house earlier to pick up a pair of shoes for you but the back door was locked.'

'Jake.' Rebekah shrugged.

'I figured as much. You get changed and I'll pop over and get a pair now. He should be home but give me your keys in case he's still at the clinic.'

When she'd gone, Rebekah slipped out of her pyjamas and pulled on the dress. The straps were two inches wide in a zig-zag pattern with a band of diamantés in the middle. The neckline also had a zig-zag pattern which came across the top of the bust, glittering diamantés again highlighting the unusual cut. It came to mid-thigh and showed off her legs to perfection.

Thankfully, Gillian had bought the next size up from what Rebekah usually wore so when she zipped it up, it didn't pull across her bust. She'd already expressed milk after the last feed just in case Anabella should wake up hungry while she was gone.

She looked down at her sleeping daughter. 'Oh, baby. You are so beautiful. Sleep well for Mummy while I'm gone. I'll be back. I promise. I will *never* leave you and I will love you forever.'

Tears blurred in her eyes as she said the words—words which had never been said to her by either of her parents.

Now, at least, she had the satisfaction of saying them to her own child.

Gillian rushed back into the room, stopping still as she gazed at Rebekah. She shook her head. 'Even without the hair and make-up, you look incredible. He isn't going to know what hit him!'

They set to work, piling Rebekah's hair on top of her head and curling the ends slightly, leaving a few loose tendrils coming down. 'I have another surprise,' Gillian announced, after she'd finished Rebekah's make-up. She pulled out a jeweller's box.

'This is a gift from Leo.'

'Leo?'

'He came by the surgery today for a check-up and when he found out what was going on, he came back this afternoon with this box. They're only on loan as he wants to pass them on to his new great-granddaughter but for tonight he insisted you wear them.' Gillian handed it to Rebekah who opened it slowly. A row of diamonds winked back at her. The necklace was classically stunning and came with a matching bracelet and a pair of studded earrings.

'Oh! I can't.'

'Yes, you can. Leo will be very upset if you don't wear them tonight. They were his wife's and he can think of nothing more fitting than for you to be adorned with them on your special night.'

'But—'

'Quit it, Becky. Jake will be here soon. He arrived home just as I left. Now turn around so I can fasten these in place.'

Rebekah did as she was told. She wanted to weep with joy at the way her friends loved and accepted her.

'Promise me one thing,' Gillian said.

'What?'

'That you'll forget about the past and the future tonight and just live in the moment. Let the night unfold and just go with the flow.'

'I don't know—'

'You need this, Rebekah. You've never had a special night like this in the entire time I've known you. Tonight you are Cinderella, going to the ball. Let it flow.'

Rebekah dragged in a deep, unsteady breath and smiled at her friend.

'I'll try.'

Jake drove his car to the hospital, furious with himself for being late.

He'd called Monica to let her know the clinic had run late and to pass on a message to Rebekah. It was almost seven-thirty!

He parked the car, cut the engine and rushed into the hospital. When he arrived at Rebekah's room, it was to find her dressed in a robe, sitting up in bed feeding Anabella. He stopped and stared, their gazes meeting.

Her sleek black hair was on top of her head in a pile of curls and diamonds seem to twinkle around her neck and ears. She looked…sexy! Wholesome and irresistibly sexy. He swallowed over the dryness of his throat. Perhaps this night together had been a mistake to organise. Just the two of them! What had he been thinking?

'Sorry. She woke and was hungry so I thought it would be best to feed her. Will this affect your plans for this evening?'

He gulped as he took a few steps into the room and then stopped. The urge to crush her to him and plunder her mouth was almost too great for him to control. He swallowed again.

'No. I've called the restaurant to let them know but they

understand how it is and will hold the table for as long as we need it.'

'Good. She's almost finished.'

The room was plunged into silence again and Rebekah began to feel a little uncomfortable. Why didn't he come into the room? Sit down? Say something? She glanced up at him to find him intently watching them. When Anabella had finished, Rebekah closed her robe and handed him the baby.

'Here's a towel. Would you mind burping her while I go and get changed?'

'Sure.' He walked to the bed and sat on the end, glad Rebekah was leaving the room for a moment. Hopefully, he'd be able to get himself under control again. 'You're worse than your mother,' he muttered to Anabella as he rubbed her back soothingly. 'Irresistible and highly kissable.' He pressed his lips to her head as though to prove his point. He felt the little body relax against his and after she'd expressed her wind, Jake wrapped her up and tucked her into the cot. Then he concentrated on taking some deep, calming breaths. He was determined to be in control of his faculties when Anabella's mother returned.

'Ready?'

Jake spun around and simply stared at the woman who stood in the doorway. Where had she come from? Rebekah! Rebekah as he'd never seen her before. Dressed in the most stunning of black dresses, with diamonds everywhere and long, luscious legs. His jaw dropped open and he felt paralysed with desire.

'You're stunning,' he breathed, and, finally able to move his legs, walked to her side. 'Ready?' He crooked his arm to her.

'Thank you.' She smiled up at him and he almost capitulated. The urge to sweep her into his arms and carry her back to their house was increasing at an alarming rate.

'Ready to go?' It was Monica who broke the spell as she walked down the corridor towards them.

Rebekah cleared her throat and looked away first. 'Yes. She's fed, burped and sleeping like a baby.'

Monica wheeled the cot down to the nurses' station as the two of them walked behind. Rebekah blew her girl a kiss. 'Sleep sweet, princess.'

Jake led her out to the car and for once she was glad he'd put the soft top up. 'Are you going to be warm enough?'

'Yes. From the hospital to the car, to the restaurant, to the car, to the hospital. I should be fine.' He walked her around to the passenger side and held the door for her. 'Thank you.'

'Where are we going?' she asked as they drove along, the scent of his aftershave winding itself around her, creating havoc with her senses.

'Chateau Yalmena.'

'Oh, they have a lovely restaurant there, or so I've heard.'

'Never been?'

'No.'

He smiled. 'I'm glad tonight is the first time.'

Everyone looked at them as they walked in, a few of the locals dining there even clapped. She smiled back and allowed herself to be seated. 'This is lovely, Jake. Thank you.'

'You're welcome.'

Settling her racing heart down to a normal rhythm, she smiled across the table at him, determined to follow Gillian's advice and enjoy every moment they had together. They talked on a variety of topics while they ate. She loved listening to Jake's stories of his youth, laughing at the silly things he'd got up to.

After dessert and one cup of coffee, which had Rebekah savouring every drop, they made their way back to the car.

'It's been a lovely evening.' Rebekah sighed wistfully. 'Thank you, Jake. You can't know how much a night out like this means to me. In fact, I can't recall ever having been out on a night like tonight.'

'But wait,' he said with a mischievous grin. 'There's more.' He held his car keys out to her. 'Time to have that drive you've always wanted.'

'I get to drive!'

'Yes. If you feel up to it,' he added.

'Are you kidding?' Rebekah couldn't stop the smile from lighting up her face. She took the keys from him and climbed behind the wheel, adjusting the seat and mirrors. 'Wow. This is even better than I imagined.'

Jake laughed. 'You really are a rev-head at heart.'

Rebekah joined in and, after securing her seat belt, started the engine. 'Oh, this is *really* nice.' She pulled onto the road, relishing every moment. 'Jake,' she said a few minutes later, 'this is so…cool. It's like the cherry on top.'

'I'm glad.' He was surprised how much pleasure he received simply from making her happy. Finally, she had that smile, the smile of pure happiness he'd seen in her eyes in her wedding photo, and *he* was the person who'd put it there.

'Go left up here,' he said.

'Hey, I'm the one who usually gives the directions.'

'Not tonight.'

She made the turn. 'Where did you want to go?'

'To the lookout.'

'Mengler Hill?'

'Yes. Gillian mentioned it today. She said it was terrific

at night and, as you can see already, we have lots of stars and an almost full moon. Besides, I told Monica I'd have you back by ten o'clock and it's only half past nine.'

She drove the Jaguar up the hill and parked in the car park. Jake came around to the driver's side to help her out. 'I'm not pregnant any more, Jake. I can get out of the car by myself.'

'I know…but a gentleman always escorts his date.'

'Is that what I am tonight? Your date?'

A low stone wall was in front of them and Jake led her over to it. They both sat down on the wall, gazing at each other rather than the stars. He brushed his fingertips across her cheek. 'You really do look extraordinarily beautiful tonight, Rebekah.'

'Thank you.' She dipped her head slightly, hoping he wouldn't see how much his words had pleased her. 'You don't scrub up too bad yourself.'

'You've seen me in a suit lots of times.'

'Yes, but tonight you're looking…I don't know… different. Handsome different.'

'So I don't look handsome at other times?'

She laughed. 'That's not what I meant and you know it. There's something…different about you tonight. I think it might be more in your eyes rather than what you're wearing.'

His gaze was intense. 'I don't want to hurt you,' he said softly, and Rebekah's heart was pierced by his tenderness. Again, he brushed her cheek with his hand before cupping her face and drawing it closer to his own. When his lips met hers, Rebekah sighed into the kiss.

His mouth was soft, gentle, as though she'd break if he exerted any more force. He made her feel precious, treasured and…special. When he kissed her like this, it gave her hope that she might one day be able to trust another man, and she desperately wanted that man to be him. Still…she had doubts.

Pushing the thoughts away, she concentrated on the feelings he was evoking. Some had lain dormant for years, others had never existed—until now. It was amazing how he could do this to her, affecting her until all rational thought had disappeared and all that existed was the two of them and the excitement they made together.

He pulled away and gazed at her before gathering her closer in his arms. When he felt the coolness of her skin, he pulled back, took his jacket off and draped it over her shoulders. 'Not that I want to cover up your exquisite dress but neither do I want you to get sick. Monica, not to mention Gillian, would have my hide.'

Rebekah nodded, unable to speak. Her emotions were so overpowering, so overwhelming, she wasn't quite sure how to cope with them. Instead, she took delight in being drawn into his embrace, of resting her head against his chest and savouring the scent of him. She closed her eyes, memorising everything she could, filing it away to take out one day in the future when her life might not be so perfect as it was at this moment.

'The stars in Sydney don't shine as bright as here.'

The pounding of his heart was slowly returning to normal, just like her own. 'Yet they're the same stars,' she murmured, opening her eyes. 'Out here, in the open where there aren't so many artificial lights to interfere, the stars *should* shine bright.' She paused for a moment before asking, 'Do you like it here? In Tanunda, I mean?'

'Yes, I do. It's a beautiful place.'

'And your blood pressure? Has that decreased? Have you unwound, relaxed?'

He breathed in deeply and slowly exhaled. 'See that? I could never fill my lungs so deeply back in Sydney.

Here…the pace of life is slower. Sometimes it does frustrate me—'

'How?'

'With clinic and things like that. I'm used to having every service at my disposal yet here I have to wait extra time for results while they're sent to Adelaide. Things like that.'

'But you are adjusting, aren't you?'

'Yes. I suppose you're used to it.'

'Yes.' Another pause. 'What made you so stressed in the first place? Was it just work?'

'The juggling act. I have a private practice which consists of three full days' consulting. I consult at the public hospital, I lecture at the medical school, I'm on committees at the hospital. Add to that my research project and the fact that I would like to be head of paediatrics next year and it amounts to an enormous amount of stress.'

'But you don't smoke, you don't drink excessively.'

'All things in my favour but I also don't get as much time to exercise as I would like. I was eating at odd times and never complete meals as I wasn't that hungry.'

'And so you had a mild heart attack.' An involuntary shudder ripped through her as she said the words.

'Yes. Thankfully, I was at my parents' house when it happened so my dad was able to take care of me.'

She hugged him tighter. 'Must have scared the life out of your mother.'

'Scared the life out of all of us.'

Rebekah closed her eyes at his words, cross with him for putting himself through that much pressure. 'Thankfully, you're heeding the warning and slowing down.'

'It isn't easy.'

'I don't imagine it is.' She breathed in the scent of him again. 'You *must* make sure it doesn't happen again, Jake.'

Rebekah pulled back and looked at him. '*Promise* me. When you return to Sydney, promise me you'll take it easy.'

Jake was touched by the urgency in her tone.

'When you go back, you'll still be consulting both privately and publicly. You'll still be doing your research and if you get the promotion to director—which I'm sure you will because your credentials are excellent—that will probably add even more to your load. You may be slowing down now but once you return, the pace is bound to catch up with you again—*if you let it*!'

'I know.'

'You have to be conscious of your time, the workload you'll be juggling and the demands that will place on your body. It didn't let you ignore it before and it won't again. Oh, promise me, Jake.'

She was almost wild with urging. Jake shifted back and cupped her face in his hands. 'You care that much?'

'Of course I care and not just because you're a colleague or because it's the professional thing to do. I care because I *care* for you. *Deeply.*'

'How deeply?' He gazed down into her eyes. 'Deeply enough to take a chance? Only a few weeks ago you were tarring all men with the same brush. No man could ever be trustworthy in your eyes after what Guy did to you and it's quite understandable. Your faith in my sex had shrunk to non-existent.'

'Not non-existent,' she replied with a sigh.

'But, still, you have those experiences in your life now and they're bound to affect the way you see me.'

'They do. There's a part of me which cries out to run away from you and keep on running, knowing you'll hurt me in the end. Yet another part—a new part—is urging me forward, bringing me every day one step closer to realising you just might be different from the rest. However, that doesn't stop me from caring about you.'

Jake looked down into her eyes before a small smile tugged at his lips. 'You're right.' He shook his head slightly. When had it happened? How had she become so incredibly special to him in a matter of weeks?

'Bek.' He lowered his mouth to hers, intent on showing her that he, too, cared for her.

Once again his mouth was tender, caressing hers and making her feel cherished. It wasn't an emotion she was used to experiencing but it was definitely one she could get used to. Then, without warning, something inside him seemed to snap as he dragged her as close as possible.

'You smell incredible. Like a rose garden, so fresh and vibrant. I can't get enough of you.'

The need he'd been smothering deep, down inside surged to the surface and there was nothing he could do to stop it. He wanted this woman. The desire was so powerful, so strong, he had no idea how to control it, which was definitely a first for him. He seemed to be experiencing a lot of 'firsts' with Rebekah and the sensations were knocking him off balance far more than he liked. Still, there was nothing he could do about it—especially when he was holding her so close.

Her scent had wrapped itself around him, much the same way his arms were wrapped around her. They were locked together in an electrifying embrace, one so hot he was sure they'd sizzle and steam if the heavens opened up and poured rain down on them.

Never in her life had she felt this way. Her appetite for him appeared to be voracious and uncontrollable. How in the world was she supposed to let this man go? She knew it was inevitable, she knew the day would come when he would walk away from her. No. Not now. She wouldn't think about that now, not when his mouth was hot on hers, not when her heart was pounding with unbelievable joy. She needed to enjoy this moment in time. This was what she'd craved almost since the first moment she'd laid eyes on him.

He shifted slightly and brought first one arm, then the other beneath the jacket which sat on her shoulders, ensuring it didn't fall off with the movement. He groaned as he slowly slid his hands around her waist, his thumbs gently caressing the undersides of her breasts before continuing around to draw little circles at the base of her spine. Now there was only one barrier separating him from the touch of her skin and for the moment he could live with that.

He broke free, just for a second, both of them breathing heavily, their hearts tattooing out a wild and unsteady rhythm. He pressed small butterfly kisses to her cheek, down to her ear where he nibbled for a brief moment before continuing down to her neck.

She arched back slightly, giving him access to what he'd been coveting for weeks. Even the necklace she wore didn't deter him, even though he wished it were gone. She laced her fingers into his hair, revelling in the fact that she was finally allowed to touch him in this familiar way, to feel the soft strands of his dark brown locks smooth against her fingertips. His head dipped lower still, the kisses warm against the cool air which circulated around them, as he made his way to the top of her chest.

Up and down, along the zig-zag of her dress, he tenderly placed his lips—his hands now spanning her midriff, his thumbs repeating the action they'd performed earlier. She gasped as her body responded, a heat burning right through her—and then she felt it. That strange, new sensation which happened to breast-feeding mothers.

'Whoa!' She quickly took two steps away, severing the embrace. 'Stop.'

'What?' He looked at her with dazed confusion. 'Are you all right? I didn't hurt you?' He took a step closer and reached out a hand to her. Rebekah melted at his concern and smiled, putting her hand in his.

'I'm fine. Really, I'm fine.' She sucked in air, trying to steady her heart rate, but she was feeling the cold without his body there to shield her. 'It's just that…' She took a steadying breath. 'I'm…' Oh, this was so embarrassing. 'I'm…leaking.'

She watched as his gaze flicked to her breasts in alarm before meeting her gaze once more. A smile started to twitch at the corner of his lips as he squeezed her hand.

'Um…sorry.'

She watched him carefully, unsure *what* he was apologising for. 'Don't apologise. I guess I'm just not used to…well…everything.'

'I think we both got a little carried away.' He raked his free hand through his hair where her own fingers had been only moments ago.

Rebekah laughed. 'This is certainly a memorable end to the evening.'

'Yes.' When he saw her shiver, he escorted her to the car. 'Pumpkin time.'

'Yes,' she agreed, glad of the car's instant protection from the wind. He walked around to the driver's side and climbed in, starting the engine and switching on the heater. He didn't make any move to drive.

'It really is beautiful up here.'

'It's one of my favourite spots.'

'I can see why. The whole valley—the parts I've seen—is charming.'

'But…?'

'But it's not my home.'

'I know,' she said softly. He was only on loan. It was a stark reminder and, regardless of whether or not she could bring herself to completely trust him, he was still only on loan. He had another life, one without her, without Anabella, and he had every right to return to it at the end of his contract. She needed to remember that—or her heart would get broken yet again.

'I heard what you said, Bek. When I return to Sydney things will start to get hectic again and I will do my best to make sure I get control of them. My parents, especially my mother, will be there, making sure I don't overdo it.'

Rebekah smiled, thinking of Deliah fussing around her son and Jake getting lovingly annoyed with her. 'I can just see it now. Deliah coming to the hospital on a cold winter's day, bringing you hot chicken soup and spoon-feeding you at your desk—*just* so she knows you're eating right.'

Jake laughed. 'You're probably not far wrong.' The laughter faded and the atmosphere became serious once more. 'Thank you for caring. It *does* mean a lot to me.' He took her hand in his and gave it a little squeeze. 'You've become important to me in many ways, Bek—hard to believe in such a short time—but our lives are on different paths regardless of the attraction between us.'

She nodded sadly. 'I know. The attraction between us is sometimes…uncontrollable.'

'You can say that again,' he mumbled, and shook his head.

'But you're right. We have different lives waiting for us. Speaking of which, we'd better get back to the hospital. Anabella might be ready for a feed.'

'Of course.' He let go of her hand and manoeuvred the car out the exit and down the hill to the town below. Both were silent on the five-minute drive before he pulled the car up outside the hospital.

Jake came around and opened the door for her, drawing her close as soon as he could.

'I had a good time tonight,' she said softly. 'Thank you. It was an amazing evening, especially getting to drive your car.'

Jake chuckled. 'I'm glad it made you happy.' He leaned forward, cupped her face in his hands and brought his lips down for one last kiss. The instant his lips brushed hers, she closed her eyes, savouring the touch.

'Get inside before you get too cold,' he whispered. 'Give Anabella a kiss from me.'

'I will.' Gradually, she stepped from his embrace, handing back his jacket. 'Thanks for the loan.' She continued to move back.

'My pleasure.'

She didn't want to go—didn't want *him* to go, and the surge of need surprised her. It was no good, she reminded herself. They were destined for different lives—different paths—different loves.

CHAPTER EIGHT

'HI.' REBEKAH opened the door to let Gillian in. 'We were going to come across to the clinic later today for the check-up. I even rang to make an appointment with Nicole and she told me I was being ridiculous.'

Gillian laughed as she came in and sat down at Rebekah's kitchen table. 'She told me. You should know by now that you don't need to make an appointment in your own practice.'

'Well, I thought I should do things by the book. You know, no preferential treatment.'

Gillian laughed again. 'You really haven't been getting much sleep, have you? That's the only reason I can come up with as to why your brain's gone soft. Preferential treatment, indeed. Who else *should* get it?'

Rebekah gazed down at Anabella, sleeping peacefully in the bassinet. 'I'm actually getting more sleep now than I was before I had her.'

'Exactly. I firmly believe that the last few weeks of pregnancy are really preparing you for the next few years of your life. You know, coping with broken sleep, being able to get back to sleep quickly, coping with exhaustion, not to mention the toilet issue.'

'What toilet issue?'

'Well, when you're heavily pregnant, you know where all the public toilets are and then when you're toilet-training your child you already know the quickest and most direct route to each and every public toilet in town.'

Rebekah laughed. 'You always give such great advice. Cuppa?'

'That would be lovely.'

'Busy clinic?'

'Yes. Jake's doing the afternoon clinic and I'll do the house calls. I came across not only to check on how you were both doing but to ask if you'd like to come along.'

Rebekah found it hard to curb her disappointment. 'Of course,' she said softly, and forced a smile. 'We'd love to come.' She turned away and concentrated on filling the kettle and switching it on.

'Things still aren't going well between you and Jake?'

Rebekah looked at her friend. 'No, but, then, it's better this way.'

'What's that supposed to mean? I thought you two had a good time when you went out for dinner. Now it appears you've both started avoiding each other again.'

'Not so much avoiding but…' She shrugged. 'Well, yes, I guess you could say avoiding.'

'What about Anabella?'

Rebekah smiled and looked at her daughter. 'I doubt she'd let *anyone* ignore her. No. Jake is firmly wrapped around her little finger and he appears quite happy there.' She took two mugs down from the cupboard and rummaged around for the teabags and sugar.

When she didn't say anything further, Gillian prompted, 'I'm not leaving until you tell me what's going on.'

'You want the post-mortem of my date with Jake?'

'Absolutely. It was a week and a half ago and you've remained amazingly tight-lipped about it.'

Rebekah came and sat at the table again. 'It was a wonderful, romantic night—the best I've ever had. And the worst.'

'What happened?' Gillian was concerned as well as antsy. 'Come on, girl. Spit it out.'

'I realised the truth.' There was sadness in her eyes as she spoke. 'We're from different worlds. Regardless of how I feel about him or what he might feel for me, it isn't going to work. He will return to Sydney when his time here is done. It's where he belongs.' Why was her voice getting all choked? 'I know this is the way it has to be. I know this is the right thing to do. I need to save my heart from further damage, I need to withdraw from Jake, to keep my distance.' Rebekah looked down at her hands. 'I only hope Anabella won't be too unhappy when he eventually leaves. I guess that's what concerns me most. I know she'll only be a few months old but it's as though she has this invisible bond with him. Every single time he holds her she stops crying. It's amazing.'

'Let me check I have this straight. You're keeping your distance because he'll eventually leave,' Gillian stated.

'Yes.'

'Do you trust him?'

Rebekah stood and finished making the tea, bringing the cups back to the table before she answered. 'I trust him on several levels. That only surprises me. I didn't think it would be that easy to trust again, but where my heart is concerned the question of whether or not he would be faithful…well…I don't know. I certainly *hope* he would.'

'He doesn't seem the type,' Gillian said.

'And Guy did, I suppose.'

'Yes. Guy wanted adventure and glamour and prestige. He was selfish, Becky, and I know you've acknowledged that. Jake…he's not like that and I think you've acknowledged that, too.'

Rebekah sipped her tea, a thoughtful frown creasing her forehead. 'You're right, of course. I have realised that but

I still don't know if I can take that first wobbly step forward to putting my happiness, and Anabella's, into Jake's hands.'

'Don't you think he'd make a good father?'

'I think he'd make an excellent father—if he took the time out of his busy schedule to enjoy his family. Towards Anabella he's never been anything but loving and caring. He's even changed a few of her nappies.'

'Wow.'

'Tell me about it. He's happy to hold her, look after her, especially if I need to have a shower or if I'm on the phone with a patient. The other night, I was sitting in the lounge, feeding her, and he came in and sat with us.'

'That's promising.'

Rebekah shook her head. 'He asked polite, medical questions about how she was doing, feeding and that sort of thing. When she was finished, he offered to burp her and when she dozed off to sleep, he checked her over—even got his stethoscope and listened to her heart—and then, when he was satisfied, he left. I think if she'd been awake, he might have stayed, but in staying we would have wound up in a tense and troublesome situation and I think that's what we're both *really* trying to avoid, rather than each other.'

Gillian sighed. 'What on earth are you going to do? The man's here for another five months, Becky.'

'I know and I've been thinking about that. I mean, we could alter his contract. He doesn't have to stay the full six months we initially agreed on.'

'You're not ready to come back to work. I won't allow it.'

'Not full time but definitely part time or even three-quarter time.'

'Three-quarter time? Will you listen to yourself? Your daughter is only two weeks old.'

'Yes, and she's a good baby. She sleeps well, she feeds well and she's no trouble at all.'

'If you come back to work too early, you might have to stop breast-feeding or your milk might dry up.'

'I've thought of that. Why couldn't I bring Anabella into work with me? She can sleep in the reception area with Nicole and I'll be available for feeds. Trust me,' she went on quickly, noticing the look of scepticism on Gillian's face, 'the patients won't mind waiting if Anabella needs feeding. They all adore her, and that way everyone can see her when they come to the clinic.'

'What if she needs changing? Or she's sick? Nicole can't look after that. Besides, it's a medical clinic, Becky, not a childcare centre.'

'All right. How about this? I find someone to look after her here, at home. I'm only working across the road so I can pop home whenever I'm needed, for feeding and stuff like that.'

Gillian shook her head and said softly, 'Is it really *that bad*? This time you have now with Anabella won't come again. She'll never be this little again, Becky, and I don't want you to miss it. Are things really *that bad* with Jake that you need to risk this precious time?'

Rebekah slumped forward onto the table in defeat. 'I have to find a way to cope without him, Gillian, and the only way I can see that happening is if he leaves. I know he's as uncomfortable with things as I am and, to be honest, I can't take any more of his extreme politeness.' She lifted her head. 'When he kisses me, I…' She sighed with longing. 'I can't concentrate. I can't think. Everything—and I mean *everything*—gets wiped out of my mind. There is only him and me and nothing else and that scares the living daylights out of me. I just want to stay in his arms for ever.

Gillian's laugh was full of sympathy. 'You do have it bad, don't you?'

'Yes,' she mumbled, her heart searing with pain. 'How am I going to survive?'

'You just will. I know it and I'll tell you how I know it. It's because you're a survivor, Becky. Look how far you've come. First your parents, then Guy—and you're still standing.'

'You think so?'

'I *know* so.'

'Some days it doesn't feel like it.'

'I know.' Gillian placed her hand over Rebekah's and gave it a squeeze. 'You'll get through it—and your friends will help you.'

Rebekah smiled. 'Thanks.'

The phone on Jake's desk rang the instant his patient had left.

'Jake,' Nicole said, 'I have a call for you from Sydney.'

'Thank you. Put it through.' He waited until he heard the click signalling that Nicole had hung up. 'Dr Carson.'

'Jake.'

'Mum.' Although he loved his mother most dearly, he simply wasn't in the mood for a chat. She'd ask about Anabella and Rebekah and right now they were two women he didn't want to think about.

'How is everyone?'

'Good.'

'Anabella? How is she?'

He smiled involuntarily. 'Growing and changing every day. It's amazing to see. She's so small and beautiful.'

'You sound as though you're smitten.'

'I am.'

'And what about with Becky?'

Becky! Jake shook his head. His mother and Rebekah were becoming way too familiar for his liking. He knew Rebekah liked talking with his mother and as she'd never really had a mother who cared for her, he supposed he could understand the appeal.

'Jake? Are you still there?'

'Yes, Mum.'

'Are you going to answer the question?'

'No, Mum. How's Dad?'

His mother sighed at the change of subject. 'Good. Picking up nicely. Driving me insane.'

Jake chuckled. 'He *is* getting better, then.'

'Listen, dear. Another reason for this call is to remind you of the dinner on Saturday night.'

'What dinner?'

'Just as I thought. Your father is being honoured by the Society of Obstetricians on Saturday night.'

'That's *this* Saturday?' he asked incredulously.

'Yes, dear. Black tie. Bring a guest if you feel like it.'

'Uh…I'll need to check with Rebekah and Gillian. How could I have forgotten?' He shook his head in disgust. An all-important night in his father's life and he'd almost forgotten it.

'You've had other things on your mind, dear. Don't worry about it. Also, Aaron Libskee and his wife came to dinner the other night, just a casual thing, you know. Did the world of good for your father. Anyway, he thought if you were in Sydney this weekend, he'd catch up with you on Friday afternoon about your research project.'

Jake was stunned. Not that Professor Libskee wanted to meet him but that he hadn't thought about this proposed meeting, or his research project, for quite a while. How had that happened? He was one hundred per cent committed to that project. How could he have forgotten?

'*This* Friday?'

'Yes. Is that a problem? Because I'm sure it can be changed.'

Today was Monday and he mentally went through things. 'No. It's sooner than I anticipated. I'll reorganise my schedule for Friday and fly to Sydney on Thursday night.' The intercom on his desk buzzed. 'Listen, Mum, my next patient is here. Thanks for the information and I'll give the professor a call and discuss the meeting with him. Give my love to Dad.' He waited for his mother's farewell before disconnecting the call. He raked a hand through his hair and stood, then paced around his office. How could he have forgotten about his research project? Sure, he'd started collating the information Guy had collected but it was nowhere near finished. His mind raced though everything he'd have to do between now and Friday. His research deserved his attention and he'd been neglecting it far too much.

Now, though, he needed to come up with some good ideas to revamp the research project and he needed to do it before Friday. The project was only in its preliminary stage. This meeting could take it further, make it national.

Jake was sure if he explained the importance of this meeting to Rebekah, she'd understand. Depending on the outcome of the meeting, he might need to break the contract he had here. It wasn't something he liked doing but, given their present circumstances, she might actually want it as well. Definitely something for him to think about in more detail.

Rebekah.

Jake breathed in deeply, filling his lungs completely. Both she and her daughter were becoming far too important to him and he had to pull away. He shook his head, still uncertain how he'd come to find himself in such a predicament. He definitely had feelings for her but how had they escalated so quickly? The woman was driving him insane. He hardly slept at night and it had nothing to do with little Anabella waking up for feeds. His sleeplessness had started long before she'd been born. In fact, he couldn't remember having one decent night's sleep since he'd arrived in Tanunda. At first he'd told himself it was the change from his inner city apartment but now he acknowledged the truth. It was Rebekah.

He was relieved he'd switched duties with Gillian for this afternoon because it meant he didn't have to spend time fighting the urges to haul Rebekah into his arms. She had been too tired to accompany him last Monday but this week he knew she was ready to get out and show off her baby.

The town's people weren't so bad, a little nosier than he was used to but it added to the rural charm. Several of his patients had asked about his date with Rebekah but when he'd answered politely that Rebekah had seemed to relax and enjoy herself, they'd been satisfied.

Jake raked a hand through his hair in agonising frustration. The question was, what was he going to do about it? Would it be better for them both if he asked to be released from his contract? The last thing he wanted to do was to leave her in the lurch. Anabella was a good baby and had a plethora of people to look after her but would Rebekah cope being away from her baby? She'd probably do it if she had to, but she would prefer not to.

He shook his head, amazed at how well he knew her. In a few short weeks he'd come to feel such a passionate regard for her and her physical and mental well-being was vitally important to him… Then again, so was his own self-preservation.

The intercom buzzed again and he turned his head sharply. 'Yes, Nicole?'

'Your next patient is here.'

'Thanks. Send them in.'

Jake glanced around his consulting room and it was then he realised the main issue. Did he *want* to go back to Sydney? He hadn't thought he could be happy here in Tanunda and although he was reluctant to admit it...he was.

No!

He was thinking with his heart, not with his head. Thinking with his heart would cause him nothing but trouble. The meeting with Libskee would clarify things—of that he was certain—so once his next patient had left, he would contact the airlines and book a ticket to Sydney for Thursday night.

Sydney would be good for him.

Sydney would ground him back in reality.

CHAPTER NINE

'SYDNEY!' Rebekah stood from her chair in surprise, almost knocking over her drink.

'Yes.'

'*This* Thursday night?'

'Yes.'

'That's only three days.'

'Yes.'

Rebekah forced herself to calm down—forced the instant surge of alarm which had ripped through her body to dissipate. She sat at the table and tried to think rationally and calmly. Questions flooded her mind. Why did Jake need to go back? Why so urgently? Were his parents all right? Had something else happened to his father? Had something happened regarding his research project or the position for director of paediatrics?

'I know it's short notice and I apologise but, you see, I'd forgotten my father was being awarded a special honour on Saturday night. The Society of Obstetricians,' he added.

'Oh!' Relief flooded through her. His parents were fine. Her breathing slowed to a more even pace, although that still didn't explain why he needed to leave here on Thursday night. Still, it was none of her business. 'I don't perceive a problem. It's only the clinic on Friday that will need to be covered and I'm sure Gillian and I can work something out.'

'Thanks, Rebekah. I really appreciate it.' He shook his head. 'I can't imagine how I'd forgotten about Dad's thing. It's been planned for months.'

'You were recovering from a heart attack, Jake.'

'*Mild* heart attack,' he interjected.

Rebekah smiled. 'Sorry, but it's understandable, Jake.' She drained her cup and carried it to the sink. 'At least you'll be able to check up on him, see how he's getting along, although your mother did say they'll be taking the cast off some time next week. What time does your flight leave on Thursday?'

'Seven o'clock from Adelaide.'

'Right. We'll make sure you finish afternoon clinic early enough so you can drive down to catch your flight.' He'd been leaning against the bench while they'd talked—keeping his distance from her, no doubt. She put her cup down and turned to face him. 'I'm sorry if I'm intruding, Jake, but why do you need to go Thursday night? It would be much better if you didn't push yourself, drove to Adelaide on Friday and caught a flight in the middle of the day.'

'I have a meeting on Friday afternoon.'

Rebekah frowned. 'Oh.'

'Regarding my research project,' he added stiltedly.

'Oh.' Her frown lifted. 'Have you managed to collate everything Guy did?'

'Almost. I'll need to get stuck into that and write up a new proposal.'

'For?'

'For the expansion of the project. Up until now, it's only been an NSW-based study, with the exception of Guy. With the work he's done, it will help show the powers that be that the project needs to be national, not just state-based.'

'How will you do that?'

'That's what I need to figure out between now and Friday afternoon.'

'I see.' The phone rang and Jake picked it up.

'Dr Carson.' He listened, his gaze meeting hers, and she

knew it was something medical. 'Right. I'll be over.' He disconnected the call. 'Amy's gone into labour.'

Rebekah nodded. 'Why don't you head over to the hospital? I'll get Anabella organised and we'll be there soon.'

'Don't disturb her. Gillian's going to meet me there.'

'I'm coming,' she said firmly.

'With Anabella? You can't take her to the hospital with you. It's cold outside.'

'Why can't I? I can bundle her up and it's just across the road. It's not raining out tonight. She'll be fine.'

Jake eyed her for a second and she felt his disapproval. 'I'm sure Gillian and I can cope without you but if that's the way you want it, so be it.'

'It's the way it has to be, Jake. Gillian may be able to deliver the baby but I'm the one licensed to do emergency C-sections. Regardless of whether or not you can *cope*, I still need to be there.'

'I guess I'll see you there, then.' With that, he walked out the back door.

Rebekah sighed and shook her head, frustrated at his high-handedness, while she raced around the house, packing the baby bag and switching off lights. Anabella slept on while Rebekah wrapped her up, cradling her close and placing her gently into the pram. The situation brought home to Rebekah just how much her life had changed. If she wanted to resume work, she was going to have to come up with a plan. Doing clinics and house calls would be fine, but emergencies? She'd have to think of something. She couldn't drag Anabella over to the hospital every time she was needed. She couldn't even leave it to Gillian to pick up the slack, even though she knew her friend would.

She glanced down at Anabella, wrapped up and ready to face the cool night air. 'Life has changed, gorgeous girl, and Mummy has to learn how to deal with it.' As she spoke the words out loud, Rebekah knew she wasn't just referring to her professional life.

When Rebekah arrived at the hospital, Monica took the pram and pushed it into the nursery. 'She'll be fine.'

'Thanks, Mon. What are you still doing here?' Rebekah blew her daughter a kiss and headed to the labour room.

'I was working late and when I heard about Amy, I thought I'd stay and help.'

'Glad you did.' When she walked into the room, Jake was hooking up the foetal heart monitor and Amy's husband, Andrew, was hovering nervously at his wife's side. 'Gillian here yet?'

'Not yet,' he answered. They listened to the baby's heart beat, sharing a look. 'It's a little slower than I'd like,' he said softly.

'Hi, Amy.' Amy was lying on the bed with her eyes closed. 'Amy?' Rebekah touched Amy's cheek but still received no response. She tapped the other woman's face. 'Amy? Wake up.'

The other woman slowly roused and sluggishly opened her eyes. 'Hmm?'

It was then Rebekah realised Amy was drunk. She glared at Andrew. 'How much has she had?'

'I...I don't know,' he stammered. 'I came home from work and she was standing in the middle of the kitchen floor in a puddle of water. It took me a while to realise what had happened and then she passed out. I managed to catch her so the baby wasn't hurt and then I got her into the car and brought her straight here.'

'Did she regain consciousness on the drive?'

'In and out,' Andrew replied.

'Monica, I want a blood test taken. Test for blood alcohol level and liver damage. Urine test as well to check for protein. How's her BP?'

Monica was just unwrapping the blood-pressure cuff. 'Two hundred over one-ten.'

'PIH.' Rebekah nodded.

'What's PIH?' Andrew asked.

'Pregnancy-induced hypertension. It means Amy's blood pressure is quite high because she's in labour.' She turned to Monica. 'Call Colin and have him come in to assess her. I don't know if he can give her an epidural until we know her blood alcohol level, so get a rush on that. Jake, status on the baby?'

'Heart rate is still low but holding steady for the moment.'

'Good. Andrew, has she had any contractions?'

'Not that I know of.'

'The alcohol might be acting as an anaesthetic so she may not be feeling them,' Jake said. 'I'll get a monitor on her so we can watch when the contractions come and the severity of them.'

'Good. Hi, Gillian,' she said when the other doctor came into the room. Rebekah gave a quick update of statistics.

Gillian nodded. 'Are her parents here yet?'

'Not that I've seen and, believe me,' Rebekah said quietly, 'we'd know they were here.' She sighed and looked over at Amy. She knew what it was like to be brushed aside by family members and where Amy had been the apple of her parents' and husband's eye *before* the baby had come along, it now seemed as though she was only a means to an end—the carrier. No wonder the woman had become depressed.

Rebekah should have tried harder to get Amy to stop drinking. 'I'll be back in a minute,' she said, and headed to the nursery to check on Anabella. Jake came in a few moments later.

'Everything all right?'

'Yes. She's sleeping soundly.'

'I'm not talking about Anabella.'

'Me? I'm fine.' She walked over to the window and looked blankly out into the dark night. 'I just can't stop thinking I could have done more to help. After the last time Amy was in hospital, I thought things were looking up. Now…now she's lying in there, completely out of it, with a husband who only seems to care for the child she's carrying.'

'It's not your fault,' Jake said. 'You may have seen Amy regularly for check-ups but you didn't pour the wine down her throat. It's a common occurrence, Bek. I've seen it a dozen times. Amy was embarrassed and didn't want you to know she hadn't been strong enough. Even the times I've seen her, she would swear she hadn't had a drink. She didn't want you to know she was struggling. She didn't want anyone to know she was struggling.'

'But we found her, Jake. We went there and she wasn't well.'

'That's right. So we admitted her and did what we thought was best. We watched her, hoping she was telling the truth, but she wasn't. Those were *her* decisions, Bek. We couldn't *force* her to do anything and we certainly didn't force her to drink as much as she's been doing.'

Rebekah closed her eyes and sighed. 'GPs need to be better informed. We need to know what to look for, we need more seminars on these sorts of things—especially for those of us in rural or country areas. We're the first point of contact and we're the ones who usually look after the patients on a day-to-day basis.' She opened her eyes and turned to face him. 'We need to be better informed.'

Jake listened to what she had to say. She was right. There was a lot of information in hospitals and city centres but they needed to broaden their horizons. 'You've raised a good point, Rebekah. I'll see what I can do. In the meantime, don't go beating yourself up over Amy.'

'Easier said than done. I've known her for years and although we've never been close friends, she was still a patient of mine and I'll always feel like I failed her.'

Jake wanted to go to her, to stop her pain, to stop her hurt, but he knew he couldn't. To touch Rebekah, even in a gesture of comfort, wouldn't get them anywhere. He'd hold her and he'd want to keep her there. He'd want to kiss her, to let her know that he was there and that he really did care.

Instead, he glanced down at Anabella as she stirred slightly but then settled back to sleep. 'I'll go and check on Amy again.'

Rebekah nodded and watched him walk away.

Three hours later, Amy's blood alcohol level was reasonable enough for Colin to attempt an epidural. She had started to feel the contractions, which was a good sign, but Jake wasn't happy with the baby's present situation.

'Deceleration on the CTG.'

'The CT what?' Andrew asked.

'The baby's going into distress.' They shared a look and with a nod Rebekah turned to Colin.

'Give me an epidural block, stat.'

The anaesthetist nodded and set to work.

'Monica,' Rebekah said, 'prep her for an emergency C-section and get the theatre ready.'

'What? What's going on?' asked Amy's mother, who was resting her hand possessively on Amy's stomach.

'The baby's not coping,' Rebekah explained.

'Not coping with what?' Andrew wanted to know.

'With everything. First of all, Amy's blood-alcohol level when she came in was point one five. That's three times the state limit for driving.'

'So? She'd had a bit too much to drink today,' her father said defensively. 'She's been drinking wine all her life. She can handle it.'

'*She* might be able to but the baby can't. Alcohol in the mother's blood crosses over to the baby through the placenta so the baby has the same blood-alcohol level as Amy.'

'Oh no.' Amy's mother turned to glare at her daughter. 'What have you done? What have you done to my grandchild?'

Rebekah watched Amy shrink and, nodding to Gillian, they quickly ushered her parents out of the room. 'I'll take care of them,' Gillian said. 'You get her to Theatre.'

'I'm not leaving,' Andrew said.

Rebekah nodded. 'We'll need you to give Amy support during the procedure.'

'What procedure?'

'The baby is in distress, Andrew. We need to get the baby out as soon as possible and Amy's blood pressure keeps climbing. Both are in danger of losing their lives if we don't act immediately.'

He paled at her words. While she'd been talking, they'd been getting Amy ready to move to the theatre. Once everything was ready, they wheeled her bed down, the machines and monitors she was hooked up to, alongside the trolley.

Soon Amy was settled on the operating table with a screen erected around her shoulders to shield her from the operation. Gillian returned to assist and, after getting the go-ahead from Colin, Rebekah made her incision and quickly pulled the baby out.

'Congratulations,' she said, holding the baby up so Amy and Andrew could see.

'A boy!' Andrew whooped. Amy merely closed her eyes

as though in pain. 'We're going to call him Nathan. Nathan James,' Andrew continued, a bright smile on his face.

'That's a lovely name,' Rebekah replied.

Jake was standing beside her, waiting with a warmed, sterile nappy to wrap the premature baby in. Rebekah placed the little boy into Jake's waiting hands. 'Forceps,' she said, and clamped the cord off with two sets of forceps, cutting the cord between them.

Jake took the baby to the neonate section trolley, Monica working beside him. Rebekah delivered the placenta before starting to suture. 'How's it going?' she asked.

Jake was rubbing the baby with one hand, stimulating the blood. 'Heart rate is low, breathing isn't too good. Monica, suction.'

Monica did as he asked while he checked the baby's reflexes and colour. 'Still quite blue. Come on, little man, come on,' he urged. He shook his head. 'We'll need to intubate. Facial features are indicative of FAS. Flat mid-face, low nasal bridge, indistinct philtrum and thin upper lip.'

'One minute,' Monica said.

'Apgar score is five,' Jake said.

'What…what's going on?' Andrew asked.

'The baby's not responding too well,' Rebekah said quietly. 'How are you doing, Amy?'

There was no reply. Rebekah looked over the screen at her patient and saw tears running down the woman's cheeks.

'Blood pressure has stabilised,' Colin reported, and Rebekah nodded.

'Colour is mildly improving,' Jake called. 'Still clinical evidence of neurological dysfunction.'

'What does that mean?' Andrew asked, looking worried.

'His reflexes aren't responding well,' Rebekah interpreted. Gillian administered an injection of vitamin K to Amy to help with blood clotting while Rebekah continued to suture. Everyone was waiting.

'Five minutes,' Monica said.

'Apgar score is four,' Jake reported.

'What is this AP thing?' Andrew asked frantically.

'It's a score we use to assess the state of wellbeing in newborn babies.' Rebekah said.

'What's it out of?'

'Ten.'

'So…so four isn't good?'

'No.' Now was not the time to lie to them, to tell them everything would be all right—because it probably wouldn't be. Rebekah's heart turned over with sympathy and pain for the new parents.

'Arrange transfer for both Amy and Nathan to Adelaide,' Jake said. 'Is there a hospital there that has a critical care unit for mothers?'

'Yes,' Rebekah replied. 'It's down south. Get someone onto it, Mon,' she said.

'I'm on it,' the CNC replied.

Rebekah was relieved Jake had been around to deal with the baby. Nothing like having their own paediatrician on tap when they needed him, and they had really needed him tonight. With his research and knowledge of FAS he knew exactly what to look for and how to deal with it. Nathan couldn't have been in better hands if he'd been in the biggest hospital in Australia.

Jake continued to monitor the baby and Amy continued not to say anything. Rebekah could almost *feel* the guilt radiating from her patient and wished there was something she could do to help. When it was time to transfer them, Jake insisted on going with them.

'Call me,' Rebekah said before he climbed into the Royal Flying Doctor's plane. 'Let me know what's happening.'

'I will,' he said, and before he knew it, she'd quickly pressed her lips to his own. He caressed her cheek before turning away, trying hard to focus on his work rather than the sad look in Rebekah's eyes.

Jake put his key in the back door to unlock it, only to find it wasn't locked at all. He ground his teeth together in frustration with Rebekah. It was two o'clock in the morning, for crying out loud. She shouldn't have the back door unlocked! What if someone had come into the house? Burgled it? She could have been hurt. Anabella could have been hurt.

He walked into the kitchen and put his keys on the table. She was going to have to change her way of thinking. She was a mother now. She had a responsibility not only to keep herself safe but Anabella as well.

He rubbed his hand across his forehead, trying to soothe the throbbing headache which only seemed to be getting worse. What a night! Jake sat down at the table and closed his eyes.

'How's Nathan?' The words were spoken softly, the concerned lilt of Rebekah's voice washed over him. He heard her sit before he opened his eyes and looked at her. She was dressed in a pair of pyjamas with her robe belted firmly around her waist. He glanced down at her feet and wasn't surprised to see those fluffy slippers she loved so much on her feet. At first he'd thought they were ridiculous, now he realised they suited her. They reflected her personality— warm, soft and comfortable. She probably wouldn't like to hear herself being described that way—what woman would? But Jake had never felt as comfortable in his life as he did when he was with Rebekah.

'Nathan…died.'

Rebekah gasped and placed a hand over her mouth. 'When?'

'Just after midnight. His brain damage was quite severe. We did a cranial ultrasound and it was…' He broke off and shook his head.

Rebekah hung her head and wrapped her arms around herself, closing her eyes as the pain of the situation hit her with full force. 'Amy?' She sniffed and lifted her head, shaking her hair back from her face.

'I told her…and Andrew.'

Rebekah opened her eyes and Jake felt his gut wrench with protectiveness at the pain and anguish he saw there.

'I don't know how she'll get through this. I don't think I could.'

'She'll need counselling, Bek. A lot more than you're qualified to give.'

'Do women in these situations ever bounce back?' Her voice was urgent, imploring, and he wanted nothing more than to tell her everything would be all right with her patient…but he couldn't and he knew she knew it.

Instead, he reached across for her hand, waiting while she placed it snugly in his. 'The death of a child is…heartbreaking, soul-destroying, regardless of the circumstances. Through drinking so much alcohol, Amy has been responsible for her son's death.' He shook his head. 'The normal level of blame and guilt a parent feels when something happens to their child is enormous but in this instance, Amy will be torn to shreds—devastated. She may suffer a breakdown, which is quite common, given the circumstances. It's different for everyone but the guilt is *always* there and can sometimes be almost impossible for people to deal with.'

Rebekah shook her head and pursed her lips, unable to stop her eyes from welling with tears that spilt down her cheeks. '*This* is what you need to put in your research project, Jake. Not only how to recognise symptoms but how to cope with the tragedy of this syndrome. If *I* can't cope with it, how on earth am I supposed to help my patients through it?' She sniffed, desperately trying to control her reaction, but it was impossible.

'Bek.' He ground out her name and in an instant he'd pushed back his own chair and tugged her up into his arms. He knew her emotions were that of a person who desperately cared about her patients, not only their medical issues but their personal ones as well. Added to that was the fact that she'd not long given birth herself. He knew she'd be thinking about how she would feel should something terrible happen to Anabella. Even as the thought passed through his mind, he felt a surge of protectiveness fill him completely. Anabella was vitally important to him, she'd become a part of him and he loved her. If anything were to happen to her…

Rebekah pulled back slightly, sniffing and rummaging in her robe pocket for a tissue. She blew her nose and looked up at him, overcome with love when she saw tears glistening in his eyes.

His hand caressed her face, tenderly brushing her hair back before he lowered his lips to hers. There was reassurance in his embrace and she closed her eyes, revelling in the emotion. She only wished it would last and last for ever.

He broke his mouth from hers, kissing her cheeks, her eyelids, her nose and finally her forehead…before he put her from him. 'I promised myself I wouldn't touch you again.'

Rebekah licked her lips and looked at him. 'I know.' She waited for a moment, watching him intently. He raked a hand through his hair and took another step away. 'It's crazy, isn't it…this thing between us?'

'Yes.' Jake turned and paced towards his end of the house. 'It's so…real. So volatile and intense.'

'Yes—but we can't, Jake. *I* can't.'

'I know.' He shook his head. 'No—why can't we, Bek? Tell me why.'

'Why? Because you'll be gone, Jake. At the end of your time here, you'll head back to Sydney to your life. You—here—in Tanunda… You're in limbo. You're just passing the time until you can get back on the merry-go-round. It's what you've been striving for all your life, it's your dream, your goal. I'm not in that picture, Jake, and although I'd love nothing better than to be with you, it wouldn't work out—for many reasons.'

'This isn't just about me leaving, Bek. You've been determined to tar all men with the same brush as Guy since I arrived. I know it's going to be hard for you to trust someone and that's quite normal but I had hoped…that somehow I'd be able to show you not all men are lying cheats. Not all men treat their wives like dirt. My father certainly doesn't and I'm sure you've picked that up from conversations with my mother.'

'I understand that, Jake, but—'

'Have I shown you that? Do you think that you could trust me?'

Jake stood at the other end of the kitchen, facing her—like a showdown at high noon. Rebekah didn't need this kind of questioning, didn't want to be put on the spot, and she certainly wasn't sure she could give him a direct answer. She glanced down at the floor before slowly returning to meet his gaze.

'Yes,' she said softly. 'Yes I think…in time…I could trust you, Jake, and that fact alone scares the living daylights out of me.' She bit her lip as it quivered, her eyes as wide as saucers—her heart on her sleeve. 'I could trust you, I *do* trust you…to a certain extent, and even that has surprised me. I trust you one hundred per cent in a professional capacity, I trust you with Anabella…' She smiled as she said her daughter's name. 'You're so good with her, so natural. You'll make a wonderful father someday.'

'And do you trust me with *you*?'

The smile slipped away and Rebekah felt the tears threatening behind her eyes, felt her throat constrict as she desperately tried to swallow. 'I don't know if I'm strong enough to do that,' she whispered—a tear escaping and sliding slowly down her cheek. 'If I take the risk, if I give you my heart, then I…I…' She shook her head, unable to continue.

'It's all right.' He wanted to go to her. He wanted it so badly and he could tell she wanted him to hold her, but both of them stood their ground. 'It was a foolish question to have asked in the first place. Goodnight. I hope you can sleep.'

Jake turned and stalked to the bathroom, stripping off his clothes. He turned on the taps and stepped beneath the spray, willing the water to soothe his aching muscles. At least he could do something about the physical aches he was feeling.

Why had it cut him straight to the heart when she'd been unable to answer that question? She was right! He was leaving in five months' time to return to his life in Sydney, and the uncontrollable chemistry which existed between them would wither and die when he left.

He scrubbed shampoo into his hair and rinsed it. Things between the two of them had gone too far, too fast, and now they were both thoroughly confused. He wrenched off the taps and towelled himself dry.

He needed to get away from here, to regroup. Sydney would be good in that respect, give them some distance, so hopefully, when he returned, they'd be able to reach a personal level where they could exist without the urge to throw their arms around each other every moment they were alone. Just the thought made the headache he'd had earlier turn into a pounding reverberation that wouldn't stop.

Once he was dressed, he swallowed some paracetamol and settled down to work. Even though it was close to three o'clock in the morning, there was no way he'd be able to sleep now. He rested his elbows on his desk and buried his head in his hands. Work. He needed to concentrate because he certainly had a lot of work to do between now and Friday.

He thought back to her suggestion—the one she'd voiced right before he'd been unable to resist kissing her—about helping doctors, and country GPs especially, to deal with the tragic effects FAS could inflict. He hadn't thought about that angle before but it would be necessary.

Jake lifted his head as he heard Anabella's cries come through the house and a smile came to his lips. The little girl certainly had a good set of lungs. A moment later she was quiet and he knew Rebekah would be feeding her.

It brought back visions of Rebekah holding the baby tenderly in her arms, her manner natural and relaxed as Anabella fed greedily at first and then slowed down to a more sedate pace as her little tummy was filled. It was a sight which had touched him so deeply inside he hadn't known that a secret place of longing had existed.

The fact that he was in love with Anabella was of little doubt. 'And what about her mother?' he whispered.

CHAPTER TEN

TUESDAY and Wednesday were a nightmare of worry for Rebekah.

She watched Jake turn back into the man he'd been the first time she'd met him. Stiff, starched and sedentary. He worked on his research project like a robot. First thing in the morning, he'd be sitting at the kitchen table, coffee-cup in one hand and sheaf of notes in front of him as he scribbled more information down.

In the evening, she'd hear him tapping way at his laptop computer, no doubt entering the data and information. It drove her crazy and on Wednesday evening she even offered to help.

'No, thanks,' he politely replied. His eating habits had changed along with his preoccupation for his work. Even the time he spent with Anabella had decreased, although Rebekah was glad he hadn't cut it out altogether.

'He's a machine,' she said, when Deliah called on Thursday afternoon. 'I'm really worried about him.'

'I can tell, dear. I am, too.'

'Have a talk with him when he gets to Sydney. I know he has this meeting on Friday and it wasn't in his original plan, but if he continues at this pace...I don't even want to *consider* what might happen. He's only had a month to slow down and while it's worked, in two and a half days he's managed to undo all of it.'

They talked for a bit longer and when Gillian popped over, Rebekah said goodbye, with Deliah promising to let her know when Jake had arrived safely in Sydney.

'How's Leo?' Rebekah asked, as she made Gillian and herself a cup of tea.

'Pain levels are controlled. He saw his oncologist yesterday and the report is favourable. Looks as though he might be going back into remission. I'm going to drop in and see him in a few minutes, just to touch base.'

'That's great news. Give him our love. How about Hetty? How's she coping, being back at work?'

'She's in her element and the ulcers are completely under control, almost non-existent. Now, what about you?' Her friend studied her closely. 'Have you been sleeping at *all*, Becky?'

'Of course I have. Anabella and I only woke from a nap half an hour ago. Didn't we, precious? Yes, we did. Yes we did.' Rebekah smiled at her daughter and kissed her. 'Care for a hold?'

'Thought you'd never ask. Hello, beautiful girl. I don't think it's *you* keeping your mummy awake at night. Hmm? We think it's Jake, don't we? Oh, you are so gorgeous.' Gillian hugged Anabella close. 'Still worried about him?'

'Aren't you? You've seen what he's like. Rushing through clinics—not so that he neglects his patients. He doesn't stop to chat any more and both Nicole and Monica have mentioned this to me. It's only been two days, Gillian.'

'He'll settle down again once he returns from this trip.'

'*If* he returns from the trip.'

'You think he might decide to break his contract? Stay in Sydney?'

'I don't know what I think,' Rebekah groaned.

Gillian laughed. 'Oh, you do have it bad.'

'He has another life, Gillian. A life without me and I'm…'

'You're worried he'll prefer it.'

'Yes. Isn't that silly? I want him but I don't want him. I'm in love with him but I'm not sure if I trust him.' She buried her face in her hands for a moment, then sighed and looked at her friend again. 'I'm also worried that even if he does stay, he'll work his way through the next five months the way he's been working his way through the past few days. He's going to make himself sick again.'

'It's his choice, Rebekah.'

'Well, it's the wrong one if it impacts his health.'

Gillian nodded and checked her watch. 'He actually should have been home by now. He was finishing up with the last patient when I came over.' Gillian handed Anabella back before taking the coffee-cups to the sink. 'I need to get going anyway because I promised Leo I'd drop in.'

The back door opened and Jake walked in, carrying what appeared to be a garden gnome under his arm. He looked at Rebekah, drinking in the sight of her. She was wearing her hair in pigtails, tied with red ribbons—exactly as she'd been on the first day they'd met. She was dressed in an old denim skirt, which revealed a generous amount of her legs, and a baggy red jumper. Her pink fluffy slippers were firmly on her feet. She looked…amazing.

His gaze devoured her before turning to the baby she held in her arms. Anabella was awake, her eyes trying hard to focus properly, her little fists waving in the air, her legs kicking the blanket undone.

'You are a wriggle-pot,' Rebekah said to her daughter before looking at Jake again. 'I'm sorry, Jake, I have to ask. Why do you have one of Clive's garden gnomes under your arm?'

Jake smiled and Rebekah felt as though the sun had just broken through the clouds. 'I'm taking it to Sydney with me. I've checked with Hetty so she knows where it is and doesn't get worried. She's quite excited really—about one of Clive's treasures being ''gnome-gnapped''.'

Rebekah shook her head in amazement. Just when she thought she had him pegged, he did something completely different. 'Clive's always wanted someone to do this.'

'You told me. So I thought I'd take this little fella to Sydney with me and take him fishing.' He held it up and Rebekah realised it was the gnome who was sitting on a rock, fishing pole in hand, string dangling from the end of the pole.

'In Sydney Harbour?'

'Absolutely. I thought a picture on the Opera House steps and one at the Harbour Bridge ought to do the trick.'

Rebekah and Gillian both laughed. 'He's going to love it,' Gillian said. 'Good thinking, Jake.' She checked her watch again. 'I'd really better go or I'll be late for Leo.'

'Oh,' Rebekah said suddenly. 'I almost forgot. Gillian, would you mind returning the diamonds to Leo? I keep forgetting to return them and it's driving me crazy.'

'Sure.' Gillian accepted the baby while Rebekah raced off to her bedroom. 'Here,' she said a moment later, handing Anabella to Jake. He quickly put the gnome down and held out his hands for the child, a loving smile on his face. 'You look as though you could do with some cuddle therapy.'

Jake accepted the child without a word and the first thing he did was to kiss her.

'Missed her today?'

'Yes. I didn't get my usual time with her this morning.'

'What about Rebekah? Did you miss her this morning as well?'

Jake met his colleague's gaze but didn't say a word.

Rebekah returned, noticing Gillian had handed Anabella

over, and gave her the velvet box. 'Tell Leo thank you. I felt just like a princess.'

'That was the idea.' She gave Rebekah another hug. 'I'll call you later. Don't work too hard, Jake.'

Once Gillian had left, Rebekah turned to Jake. 'I'll take her. You've probably got a thousand things to get finished.' She held out her hands but he didn't move.

'It's all right,' he said softly. 'I think she's almost asleep.'

Anabella was encompassed lovingly in his arms as he gently rocked her from side to side. Her daughter had *never* settled like that, so quickly and so quietly, when she rocked her. It was evident that Anabella had given her heart to Jake as much as Jake had given his to her. They made an incredible sight and as Rebekah watched them, a lump rose in her throat and the tears came to her eyes.

Jake raised his gaze and met hers. 'What's wrong?' He was instantly concerned.

'Nothing.' She shook her head, pigtails wiggling. 'She just looks so…perfect in your arms.'

'Hmm.' He broke his gaze from hers. 'I'll put her in her bassinet,' he said, and started walking towards Rebekah's room. 'That way, she shouldn't wake up.' Jake moved off quickly, leaving Rebekah to follow, and after he'd tucked the sleeping baby in, he glanced around her room. Her bed was unmade, her bin was full of tissues and…the wedding photograph had gone from her dresser. Instead, a hand-painted frame which held a photo of Anabella now had pride of place.

He was surprised at the relief that flooded through him and refused to dwell on it. He had a lot to do if he was going to make it to Adelaide in time to catch his late flight to Sydney. Jake turned to walk out of the room but Rebekah was standing in his way.

Neither of them spoke. They stared at each other, the atmosphere in the room thick with repressed words and tension. Her tongue darted out to wet her lips and Jake cleared his throat, still unable to look away. He shoved his hands into his trouser pockets, clenching them into fists to stop himself from hauling her into his arms and plundering her mouth.

It would be cruel—to both of them—if they gave in to the passion they were struggling to repress. He could see it clearly in her eyes and knew his own were a mirror image. The surge of desire he felt for her was stronger than anything he'd felt before, but what good was a physical attraction when nothing could come of it?

Jake knew Rebekah was weakening as she took a small step towards him, her gaze shifting between his eyes and his lips. Her breathing had increased and he could tell the struggle to overcome the need to touch him had almost been lost.

He *had* to break the moment and break it *now*. He cleared his throat. 'I'd...er...better get packed.'

She closed her eyes for a second and held her breath, clenching her jaw before opening her eyes and nodding. In that one instant he felt like the biggest heel in the world. Still, he had to do what he had to do.

'Slow down, Jake. I'm getting worried about you.'

'I'm fine.'

'You're not.' The words were spoken softly and were filled with her heartfelt concern.

'Rebekah.' He didn't need this. Not now.

'Take a breath, Jake. Go on, take a deep breath in, just as you have been in the past few weeks. I'll bet you're not filling those lungs completely any more.'

He did as she asked and felt the weight. It was as though his lungs were congested, the way they would be if he had a cold. His chest felt heavy and the realisation surprised him. 'So I'm under a bit of pressure at the moment. It will lift after the meeting on Friday.'

'I know but you don't have to carry this all by yourself. I doubt the professor you're meeting will think less of you if you tell him you've been unable to complete the proposal because you're recovering from a heart attack.'

'*Mild*,' he corrected. 'It was a *mild* heart attack.' He stalked past her but she was hard on his heels.

'Face facts, Jake. It was a *heart attack*. I don't care if it was mild or not. It was a warning and right now you're ignoring that warning.'

'I don't have to listen to this.' He continued walking to his end of the house.

'Yes.' She pursued him. 'Yes, you do. I'm only saying this because I'm concerned about you. You've been working so hard the past few days you've even been spending less time with Anabella, and that's not like the man I've come to know. You don't want to live like this, Jake, and you know as well as I do that that's exactly what you're going to do.'

'I've got five months until I return to Sydney.'

'That's right, and how are you and I going to get through those next five months?'

'First of all, I thought I might move out. That should certainly help my stress levels.'

'Stress levels? Because of me?' Rebekah hadn't thought of that possibility before.

'Of course because of you.' He turned to face her, raking a hand through his hair in total frustration. 'I can't be in the same room as you without wanting to drag you into my arms. I want to talk to you, spend time with you, see more of the countryside with you. Then reality settles in and I realise this isn't where I belong. I have a life, Rebekah, a life back in Sydney. My work, my research, my patients.'

'And what about your life, Jake? Where's that?'

He turned and looked out the window. He was silent for so long she didn't think he was going to answer. She was just about to leave when he said, 'I don't know.'

The love she felt for him overflowed with concern. Slowly, she walked towards him and wrapped her arms around his waist. He tensed but when she didn't move he shifted slightly so they were facing each other.

They held each other, both content just to be.

Jake had never felt comfort like this before, never felt so calm and peaceful. The world around them carried on but for this moment in time he felt, rather than knew, that everything would turn out right. Now all he had to do was to figure out which way 'right' was.

'Drive safely,' she whispered at last, and pulled back. 'We'll miss you.'

And then she walked away.

The band stopped playing and everyone took their seats again, ready for the presentation and speeches. Jake sat next to his mother who turned and smiled brightly at him.

'I'm so glad you're here, darling.' Deliah squeezed his hand delightedly. 'It means a lot to your father.'

'I wouldn't have missed it for the world.' Jake returned her smile.

'I'm glad to hear that,' she whispered as a man walked to the podium. 'You've been sitting here all night with such a long face. I guess it's probably because you're missing Rebekah and Anabella, although why you couldn't have brought them with you, I don't know.'

Everyone started clapping as the man began his speech. Jake didn't clap. He didn't listen to the man on the podium.

He merely frowned at his mother, even though she was no longer paying him attention. What did she mean, 'long face'? He'd been in quite good humour tonight, a little less jovial than usual but that was to be expected after the work he'd put in during this past week. If he *had* been a little out of sorts, then it was because of work—nothing whatsoever to do with either Rebekah or Anabella!

Jake's father was called up to the podium to receive his award. Shuffling up on his crutches, his father made it and received a round of applause. This time Jake clapped heartily, proud of his dad.

The acceptance speech was made but his father remained at the podium.

'I have an announcement to make.' He waited for quiet in the room. 'I'd like to take this opportunity to announce my retirement from public consulting. I've handed in my resignation to the hospital and in another month's time my wife and I head off on a road trip around Australia.'

There was a stunned silence for a moment before another round of applause. His father headed back to the table and Jake turned to look at his mother.

'Why didn't you tell me?'

'We wanted it to be a surprise.'

'It is. Are you both sure?'

'Yes. We want to enjoy our later years, Jake. We've worked so hard for so long, it's time we did what *we* want to do. We want to *live* life, Jake, not read about it in a magazine—which we feel we've been doing for far too long.'

'And you want to travel around Australia?'

'Yes, dear. Your father and I have been overseas many times but there are so many wonderful sights in this country that we haven't had time to visit—so now we're making the time.'

Jake nodded, absorbing his mother's words. 'Good on you.' His father finally arrived and slumped down into his chair, placing his crutches beside him.

'These things are such a nuisance. I'll be glad to get rid of them.'

Jake laughed. 'Where are you thinking of heading to first?'

'Well, I wanted to head up north to Queensland to catch the winter sunshine, but your mother's managed to persuade me to head west.'

'Western Australia?'

'Not that far west, dear,' Deliah answered. 'We thought…South Australia might be a nice place to start.'

'Ah…I see.' Jake nodded. 'Somewhere near…Tanunda?'

Deliah grinned. 'Now that you mention it, yes.'

'Do I need to find you somewhere to stay?'

'Oh, no. That's all been arranged.'

'Rebekah.' Jake shook his head. 'You told Rebekah before you told me?'

'Now, now, dear, don't get upset. I didn't tell her anything except that we might come over and visit. She was kind enough to find us a nice cottage to rent for a while. It's all booked. She knows nothing about your father retiring.'

'I could have looked around, found something for you.'

'But you don't know the area as well as Rebekah.' Deliah frowned at him, slightly puzzled. 'I'm sorry, Jake. If I'd have known it was going to upset you this much, I would have discussed it with you.'

'I'm not upset, Mum.' Jake exhaled harshly and stood. 'I'm just going to get some air.' He walked out to the balcony, the heavy glass door whooshing quietly closed behind him. The rain was pouring down which meant the balcony was deserted—thankfully.

What was the matter with him? Why was he annoyed his mother had turned to Rebekah instead of him? Her reason for doing so was true, Rebekah *did* know the place better than he did. Or was he annoyed that Rebekah seemed so well entrenched in his life? He hadn't *asked* her to be. He hadn't *wanted* her to be…but she was and he realised he *needed* her to be.

Since his return to Sydney, he'd been feeling very different. Out of place. Disconnected somehow. He looked up at the dark sky, unable to see a single star. He shook his head sadly, wondering if it was raining in Tanunda, wondering how Rebekah and Anabella were. Was she outside, looking up at the night sky, thinking about him? He could almost swear she would be.

Where was his life?

Jake shook his head. He'd thought it was here. He'd thought it was in Sydney with his work and his research but ever since he'd returned, he'd felt…displaced.

We'll miss you. They'd been the last words she'd said to him before he'd left. What he hadn't realised was how much he was missing them.

He heard the balcony door open and close and hoped it wasn't someone he had to make small talk with.

'There you are, Jake,' Deliah said. 'Are you all right?'

'I'm fine, Mum.'

His mother shivered a little and he immediately took off his jacket and draped it around her shoulders. 'Thank you. I didn't mean to upset you.'

'I know.' They were silent for a while, both of them watching the rain.

'How did the meeting with Professor Libskee go yesterday?'

'Very well. He liked all my ideas and is taking the proposal to the next level. He'll let me know in about two or three weeks' time what the verdict is, but at the moment it looks very promising.'

'That's good news. Will you have to devote extra time to the study or will the hours be the same?'

'Probably a few more hours per week will be required initially—'

'Jake.' Deliah shook her head. 'No. You're going to work yourself into an early grave and…well, it scares me.'

'I'll be fine, Mum.'

'So you keep telling me, but you're obviously not.'

'Pardon?' He turned to face his mother and was surprised to see tears in her eyes.

'Jake—take a look at yourself. What's going on, son? I only want to know because I love you.'

'Have you been speaking to Rebekah about me?'

'Of course I have. Rebekah loves you and she doesn't want to see you work yourself sick any more than I do.'

'Rebekah doesn't love me,' he scoffed.

'How do you know? Have you asked her?'

'No. Have you?'

'No, but I'm a woman, I can tell about these things. Oh, she may have a few problems to sort through, especially after what her husband did to her, but that's nothing that you can't help her through.'

'Did you talk to her about Guy?'

'Yes.'

'Did you ask, or did she volunteer the information?'

'What does it matter?'

'Mum, you've been interfering in my life.'

'I have not.' Deliah was adamant. 'I've been getting to know a very nice woman and someone I'm anxious to meet. Is she as nice in person as she is on the phone?'

Jake stared out at the rain. 'Yes. She's…' He paused. How *did* he describe Rebekah? 'She's…' He raked a hand through his hair. 'She's frustrating and annoying and caring and the most generous person I've met.'

'Sounds promising. Anything else?'

Jake took a deep breath—filling his lungs completely for the first time in days. 'And I love her.' He looked at his mother, a smile spreading across his face. 'I love her!' He laughed, amazed at how incredible it felt to say the words out loud.

Deliah hugged him close and then pulled back to look at him. 'And so what are you going to do about it?'

'Good question.'

'I already think you know the answer.' Deliah linked her arm through his. 'Come and say goodnight to your father.'

'Kicking me out?'

'Yes. I can tell you're eager to make some phone calls and change your flight reservations so you can get back to your girls.'

'Back to my girls.' He let out another deep breath. It felt wonderful!

Jake's flight touched down in Adelaide just after eight o'clock next morning and he rushed to where his Jaguar had been parked during his absence. Two more hours were ahead of him before he would be back with his girls and he couldn't wait. As the urban landscape gave way to the glorious vineyards of Tanunda, his heart leapt with the feeling of coming home.

Impatiently, he pulled the car into Rebekah's driveway and rushed to the back door, surprised to find it locked. He quickly opened the door and went inside, searching every room, but no one was home. His heart plummeted.

The phone rang and he snatched it up. 'Dr Carson.'

'Jake, it's Gillian. I'm at the hospital and saw you pull up. If you're looking for Rebekah, she and Anabella have gone to the Whispering Wall.'

'Where's that?'

'Williamstown.' She gave him directions, which he quickly scribbled on a piece of paper. He rushed out of the house and climbed anxiously into his Jaguar. He needed to find his girls.

He followed the directions, finally turning onto the road that led to the Whispering Wall. Rebekah's car was the only other one there and he parked beside it. He climbed from the car, scanning the area in search of them. The place seemed deserted.

He walked towards the cement wall, surprised to find it was a dam wall. There was no sign of them. Where were they? His heart was thumping wildly against his chest in concern.

'Rebekah?' he yelled.

'Jake?' Her voice sounded close and at the normal level. 'Jake?'

'Bek?' He spoke normally, slightly confused. 'Where are you?'

She laughed. 'You're here? I'm not dreaming?'

'No. How come I can hear you but I can't see you?'

'It's the wall. The curvature of the wall carries the sound around. Come down the steps onto the little platform.'

He did as he was told. 'This is freaky.'

She laughed again. 'I can't believe you're here.'

'Where are you?'

She ignored his question. 'Why are you back so soon? Were there problems in Sydney?'

'Yes. Big problems and only one solution. Is Anabella with you?'

'Yes. She's sleeping. What problems?'

'I missed you.'

Rebekah was stunned. 'That was the problem?' she asked incredulously.

'Yes. Rebekah, where are you?'

'First, tell me why missing us was such a big problem?'

'Because I know where my life is.' He paused, scanning the area again, but couldn't see them. 'My life is with you.'

'Who? Me or Anabella?'

Jake smiled. 'Both of you.'

Rebekah closed her eyes, her heart in her throat. 'Really?'

'I love you, Bek.'

She breathed in a ragged breath and sighed. Jake heard it. He heard the release of her anguish, of her pain, and he heard the sigh of hope.

'You mentioned a solution.'

'Tell me where you are.'

'On the other side of the gorge.'

He glanced across but couldn't see anything. The fenced walkway which stretched around the top of the dam wall disappeared behind trees.

'Jake?'

He didn't answer because he was up the steps and running around the wall. Rebekah could hear his footsteps as he came closer and pushed the pram up so she and Anabella could meet him.

The first glimpse of her renewed the love he'd been repressing for so long. Now he could give it wings as he finally reached her and hauled her into his arms. His mouth met hers, hard, possessive and urgent. He was a man dying of thirst in the desert and finally finding water. He pulled back and touched his fingers tenderly to her face, making sure she wasn't a mirage.

'I love you, Rebekah Sanderson. I love your daughter. Marry me.'

Rebekah's eyebrows hit her hairline. 'Marry you?' She started trembling. 'Jake.' She shook her head and pulled away.

'What? What's the matter?'

Rebekah turned and looked out over the gorge.

'Bek?' He placed his hands on her shoulders. 'Don't you love me?'

She turned to face him. 'Yes. Yes, of course I do but…'

It was then he saw it. The pain, the hurts, the betrayals of the past. She was scared. He relaxed, knowing this could be fixed. Jake drew her into his arms and held her close. 'I could *never* want another woman, Rebekah, because you're all I need. Well…you and Anabella.' He laughed. 'I know you're scared and you have every right to be, but you must feel how different things are this time.'

'Yes. It's *very* different. Before you left I wasn't sure if I could trust you with my heart but on Thursday night, when you weren't there, not only was the house so dark and lonely, my life was dark and lonely.' She pulled back to look at him. 'You're right. I'm scared. I'm scared to take another chance at love, at marriage—especially as I have Anabella to think about this time—but I'm even *more* scared to live my life without you.' Her lower lip trembled. 'Oh, Jake. I need you so much.'

Jake couldn't stand any more. He crushed her to him once more and pressed his mouth to hers. She was his— and he was *never* letting her go. She and Anabella were his family. His heart had known it for a while but his mind had taken a little while to catch up.

Eventually he released her and she smiled up at him. 'I still can't believe you're really here.'

'I am and I'm never leaving you again. I must have been mad.'

'You're staying? Here? In Tanunda?'

'If you'll marry me. You will, won't you?'

'Yes. I need you. I trust you.' She placed her hand on his cheek. 'I adore you.'

'Bek.' Desire sparked in his eyes. 'Marry me and do it soon.'

'Your parents arrive in four weeks' time so what if we give them a day to settle in and unpack and the following day we'll get married.'

He smiled. 'Done. Life in Tanunda. Should be good.'

'Especially for your heart. Oh, but what about your private practice and your job at the hospital and your research project? What happened at your meeting?'

Jake ticked her questions off on his fingers. 'The private practice is already employing a locum to do my work while I'm here. I've spoken to my partner and he's agreed to approach the locum to take over permanently.'

'Are you sure?'

'Yes, Bek. Next, I've officially resigned from the hospital—'

'But what about the directorship? You've wanted it for so long.'

Jake shook his head. 'I want you more. You were right, Bek. I would have returned to Sydney and worked myself into an early grave.'

'Don't talk like that.' She placed her fingers over his lips. Jake took her hand in his and kissed her fingers lovingly.

'My health and happiness are far more important than the directorship. And with regard to the research project, the meeting went very well. It looks as though I'll get the extra funding for the study and I can supervise all of it from right here in Tanunda.'

'You won't need to go interstate for meetings?'

'If I do, it will be about once a year, but with the internet and conference calls, I don't see any reason why everything can't be done from here, and I promise you, Rebekah, that if the need arises for me to travel, I'll be taking my girls with me.' He wrapped her in his arms. 'Haven't you realised yet that I mean it when I say I'll never let you go?'

Rebekah sighed, content and happy and amazed that she could feel this good. She glanced across at the sleeping baby, then back to the man of her dreams. 'I think the hospital would be happy to get a resident paediatrician. There's certainly enough work here for you.'

Anabella shifted beneath her covers, sniffling a little before starting to cry. Jake released Rebekah and hurried to her side. 'That cry doesn't sound good. Is she all right?'

'She's been a little unsettled for the past few days.'

'What?' He picked her up and kissed her forehead. 'Are you all right, my darling?'

Rebekah's heart melted. 'She'll be fine…now.'

'Now?'

'We've both been a little unsettled for the past few days. We've been fretting.'

'Fretting?'

'Over you.'

His concerned look disappeared as he held out his other arm to Rebekah. 'Come here.' He held her close. 'You'll never have to fret again. Either of you. We're a family and we'll be sticking together for ever. Now, come to the car. There's something I want to show you.'

Jake carried Anabella, who had snuggled into the crook of his arm, while Rebekah wheeled the pram. 'You brought us back a present?' she asked hopefully.

'Well…yes and no.'

'More yes than no, I hope.'

'All right,' he said when they reached the car. 'Put her in the pram for me and then close your eyes.'

'Jake?'

'Just do it, Bek.'

'Fine.' She did as she was asked and heard him open the car door. A moment later, he closed it again. 'Ready yet?'

'Yes,' he said softly.

She opened her eyes and started to laugh because he looked really silly. Jake was on bended knee, holding out Clive's garden gnome. 'You want to give me Clive's gnome? I don't think he'd appreciate that.'

'I told you I was taking him fishing. Look closer.'

She did and then gasped. On the end of the fishing line was a diamond and sapphire ring.

'I hope it's the right size but, if not, we can always throw it back and get a bigger one.'

Rebekah chuckled—amazed.

'Marry me, Bek.' He stood, placed the gnome on the ground and untied the ring, slipping it onto her finger.

'Yes.'

'It's a little big but you can choose another one.'

'I don't want to. We'll get it resized because this ring is…' She looked at it, unable to believe it was on her finger. Then she looked at Jake—her soul-mate. 'It's just perfect.'

Then Jake kissed her in such an intense and passionate way that she knew their love *would* last for ever.

'Come on. Let's go deliver Clive's gnome back to him— along with the photographs—and tell them the good news.'

'Then we can stop at Leo's on the way home—oh, and we'll have to show Gillian and Nicole. After that, we can go to the hospital.'

Jake looked down at the sleeping baby. 'Is there any way of stopping her, Anabella? If so, give me a clue.'

The baby slept on.

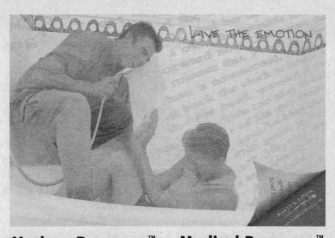

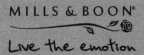

MILLS & BOON®

Live the emotion

Medical Romance™

IN DR DARLING'S CARE by *Marion Lennox*

Dr Lizzie Darling runs into her new boss, the gorgeous
Dr Harry McKay, on her first day at work and breaks his
leg! But she doesn't want to be a family doctor, or to get
involved in the tiny community of Birrini. She doesn't
want to get involved with Harry either, no matter how
attractive he is! But now, as the only available doctor,
she has no choice but to stick around...

A COURAGEOUS DOCTOR by *Alison Roberts*

Dr Hugo Patterson had his life just how he wanted it
– until a flame-haired firebrand called Maggie burst in
and turned it upside down. The sparky paramedic
found Hugo's reserved charm irresistible, and she
was determined to help him loosen up – but there
was no way the dedicated doctor would fall for
someone like her...

THE BABY RESCUE by *Jessica Matthews*

Bk 2 of Hope City

At Hope City Hospital, locum Nikki Lawrence is
taking on more than she bargained for. Not only is
she working with the man who broke her heart, she
also has to rescue a baby abandoned by its mother!
But gorgeous physician Galen Stafford still loves Nikki
beyond anything – can he persuade her that some
bonds remain unbreakable?

On sale 4th June 2004

*Available at most branches of WHSmith, Tesco, Martins, Borders,
Eason, Sainsbury's and all good paperback bookshops.*

0504/03a

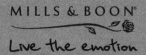

MILLS & BOON®

Live the emotion

Medical Romance™

THE CONSULTANT'S ACCIDENTAL BRIDE
by Carol Marinelli A&E Drama

An accident forces emergency nurse Leah Jacobs to
share a home with A&E consultant Cole Richardson.
His ice-cool reserve is driving her mad, but the drama
and emotion of A&E give her a glimpse of his tender
side. And then a major incident brings back memories
that Cole has buried deep inside…

THE REGISTRAR'S SECRET *by Judy Campbell*

Dr Emma Fulford was determined to be relationship-
free – so she didn't expect to fall for the infuriatingly
attractive Dr Sean Casey. But when the two registrars
had to work side by side in the hustle and bustle of
A&E, there was no way they could ignore the sparks
flying between them!

CHALLENGING DR CARLISLE *by Joanna Neil*

Dr Sarah Carlisle is in love with the wrong man – her
boss! How can she care for someone who abandoned
her sister when pregnant? Working with the devilishly
sexy Dr Matthew Bayford is a challenge, but soon
Sarah discovers he isn't as off-limits as she thought.
Her sister's baby isn't his, for a start…

On sale 4th June 2004

Available at most branches of WHSmith, Tesco, Martins, Borders,
Eason, Sainsbury's and all good paperback bookshops.

0504/03b

Next month don't miss –

SEDUCED BY A SULTAN

Enter into the fantasy, the exotic heat and the sultry passion of romance in the desert with three sinfully sexy sheikhs!

On sale 4th June 2004

Available at most branches of WHSmith, Tesco, Martins, Borders, Eason, Sainsbury's and all good paperback bookshops.

4 Books

and a surprise gift!

We would like to take this opportunity to thank you for reading this Mills & Boon® book by offering you the chance to take FOUR more specially selected titles from the Medical Romance™ series absolutely FREE! We're also making this offer to introduce you to the benefits of the Reader Service™—

- ★ FREE home delivery
- ★ FREE gifts and competitions
- ★ FREE monthly Newsletter
- ★ Books available before they're in the shops
- ★ Exclusive Reader Service discount

Accepting these FREE books and gift places you under no obligation to buy; you may cancel at any time, even after receiving your free shipment. Simply complete your details below and return the entire page to the address below. *You don't even need a stamp!*

YES! Please send me 4 free Medical Romance books and a surprise gift. I understand that unless you hear from me, I will receive 6 superb new titles every month for just £2.69 each, postage and packing free. I am under no obligation to purchase any books and may cancel my subscription at any time. The free books and gift will be mine to keep in any case.

M4ZEE

Ms/Mrs/Miss/Mr ....Initials.....................................
BLOCK CAPITALS PLEASE

Surname...

Address...

....

....Postcode ....

Send this whole page to:
UK: The Reader Service, FREEPOST CN81, Croydon, CR9 3WZ
EIRE: The Reader Service, PO Box 4546, Kilcock, County Kildare (stamp required)